NC

A CANDLE UNDER THE WATER

HEINRICH DITTRICH is a South-African writer, composer, and artist. Born in 1993, Vereeniging, his childhood was spent in Vanderbijlpark, Gauteng, until his family moved to Secunda, Mpumalanga, where he started the first grade and spent the rest of his childhood. After High school he proceeded to study languages (including, English, French, German, Latin, and Spanish) at the North-West University in Potchefstroom, North West. This opened an opportunity for him to work in France as an English Language Assistant Teacher. After traveling back and forth between the two countries, he started teaching languages at High School. He is now pursuing the arts while working as a part-time teacher.

ALSO BY HEINRICH DITTRICH

PROSE FICTION

A Candle Under the Water (2021)

POETRY

Hortus:
The Goldprint of the Arche (2023)
The Secrets of the Sacred Arms (2023)

CRITICISM

Towards Identifying a New Literary Genre: Stature—the Status (2021)
Perfeksioneer Afrikaans as Addisionele Taal (2023)

A Candle under the Water

or
LEFT

"A reminiscence of and about two parts"

By

HEINRICH DITTRICH

Edited and Introduction

by

JEANNE-MARI SPRUEW

[INDEPENDENTLY PUBLISHED]

A CANDLE UNDER THE WATER

First published in 2021

SECOND EDITION NOVEMBER 2023

Book edited by Jeanne-Mari van der Merwe

Painting by Heinrich Dittrich, Music by Heinrich Dittrich, Cover by Heinrich Dittrich

Draft2Digital

Imprint: Independently published

Self-published

To him

In loving memory of

Audrey A. DITTRICH
1958 - 2021

My dad,
who had always
the privilege to admire
my art first.

I PUT MY TRUST IN YOU, LORD!

CONTENTS

Introduction		xix
Foreword		xxiii
Prelude II		xxv
Saturn's Rings		xxvii

A CANDLE UNDER THE WATER

Prologue	A Change of Season	3
A. PERIL		5
Part 1 Winter		7
BOOK I Drean Foraged		9
Chapter One	Left Remained	11
Chapter Two	A Search for Belonging	19
Chapter Three	Time	27
Chapter Four	Time after Time	43
Chapter Five	Time after Time Again	53
Chapter Six	Love Renewed	71
Chapter Seven	A Sense of Belonging	77
Chapter Eight	Left to be Used	81
BOOK II A Dream Forgotten		91
Chapter Nine	Left to Go Away	93
Chapter Ten	A Search for Knowledge	101
Chapter Eleven	Plenty and Wealth	107
Chapter Twelve	Generation	113
Chapter Thirteen	Periodical Renewal	123
Chapter Fourteen	Liberation	129

CONTENTS

Chapter Fifteen	A Sense of Knowledge	137
Chapter Sixteen	Left Behind	143
B. HAVEN		151
Part 2 Summer		153
BOOK III A Dream Remembered		155
Chapter Seventeen	Left as Is	157
Chapter Eighteen	Engagement	163
Chapter Nineteen	Signet	169
Chapter Twenty	Fraternal	177
Chapter Twenty-One	Balance	183
Chapter Twenty-Two	Power	191
Chapter Twenty-Three	Order	197
Chapter Twenty-Four	Left up to	201
Part 3 Autumn		205
BOOK IV A Dream Dreamt		207
Chapter Twenty-Five	Left Direction	209
Chapter Twenty-Six	Decisions	215
Chapter Twenty-Seven	Consequences	221
Chapter Twenty-Eight	A Plan Set	233
Chapter Twenty-Nine	The State of Muddle	239
Chapter Thirty	The Beginning of Change	249
Chapter Thirty-One	Change	255
Chapter Thirty-Two	Left Side	259
BOOK V A Dream Re-dreamt		265
Chapter Thirty-Three	Left Someone Something	267
Chapter Thirty-Four	Chronology	275
Chapter Thirty-Five	Turning Back the Clock-Wheel	279
Chapter Thirty-Six	A Golden Age	285
Chapter Thirty-Seven	Dissolution	289
Chapter Thirty-Eight	Keeper of Time	295

CONTENTS

Chapter Thirty-Nine	Agricultural	311
Chapter Forty	From Left to Right – The Orchestrator	313
Epilogue	Spring	315

APPENDIX   317

Arne's timeline as depicted in the novel   318

Author's Notes   319

"What if this is the metaphor?"

Editor's Introduction

Life and Times

In 1993 a truly magnificent human being was born in Vereeniging, South Africa. Heinrich Dittrich grew up in Vanderbijlpark until they moved to Secunda when he was seven years of age. He started primary school in 2001 at Laerskool Goedehoop in Secunda and matriculated in 2012 at Hoërskool Hoogenhout in Bethal.

After high school he took two years off where he did a little bit of everything – playing piano, painting, writing, just to name a few. In 2015 he started his university career at North-West University in Potchefstroom, where he completed his Bachelor of Arts Degree in Language and Literature. For three years he studied, English, French and German, and for two years he studied Latin, as well as Spanish for one semester. He was also a conservatorium student where he studied piano. In 2018 he achieved his Honors Degree in French.

In 2018 he travelled to France where he worked as an English assistant teacher until 2019. In this time, he stayed in Brest. At the end of 2019 he helped as a temporary teacher at Evander High School in South Africa where I met him for the first time. Unfortunately, he had to go back to France until 2020 when Covid-19 hit, where he lived in Strasburg and commuted to Sélestat every day per train where he worked. At the end of 2020, he came back to Evander High School where he still excels as an Afrikaans teacher.

Personal Notes

Over the last two years, Heinrich became a very close friend who I value dearly. His love for art and life is absolutely inspiring. It was such a great honor the day he asked me to proofread and edit his début novel, *A Candle Under the Water*. I was amazed by the lovely story of Arné and Saturn and their incredible journey together – I can even see some of Heinrich's best qualities in these two characters; his love and care for the people he cares about, his kindness, his determination. Like Arné, Heinrich is a man you can depend on, he is always willing to help his friends, no matter how big the favour is. Like Saturn, he is very caring – on the darkest of days he is always there with a smile and a supportive hug. I can honestly say that he is the best school neighbour one can ask for. He always pops in for a quick chat, even when he doesn't know that one needs it. We share a love for good literature, art and music, and it is such a blessing to have someone so talented to talk about it with.

Heinrich, thank you so much for making me part of Arné and Saturn's love story, and this amazing project you finished. Your enthusiasm for the work you do is contagious. You are an amazing person and an absolute inspiration. Thank you for your friendship and being part of my life. I am truly blessed.

JEANNE-MARI SPRUEW, 2021
INTRODUCTION TO THE FIRST EDITION OF
A CANDLE UNDER THE WATER

Foreword

It is neither the purpose of this novel to convey in the elaboration of precise space nor to explain a particular time. But instead – when I wrote it – I reflected on time and space that are exploited to some remotest point and have ultimately become so fragile, that not even our imagination can judiciously reconcile the prominence of time and space.

Prelude II.

He's but an orphan boy, and not so born,

Left to stray, to be a waif (what false

    vow),

His saviour failed him; he's refuge, betrayed.

    Oh, how many scares it became his soul,

    How alone the feeling from pole to pole.

You might've the need to carry your own horse,

And need to drive the saddle on your'wn back,

But so, you're in command of your own course,

Your tree'll bare clusters of fruit for a snack.

    Ergo, he belongs to the Heavens

        now!

Saturn's Rings

LEGEND HAS IT THAT LONG ago, in an ancient world when times were young, and kings and queens still ruled over all the lands, there lived a poor old jeweller and his family on a farm. The jeweller struggled day in and night out to make ends meet for him and his family, but nothing seemed to come from his industriousness.

One night, however, he had a prosperous dream. A dream in which Saturn, the timekeeper, had appeared to him. It was a vision of the young and handsome god of infinite time himself. In this dream, he presented the jeweller with a gift: a ring. A precious possession that shone with bright colours of shimmering pinks, hues of grey and a hint of brown, and spiralled into seven loops. Upon awakening from his dream, the jeweller interpreted it as a sign of great fortune from the young and handsome god of infinite time himself. For this reason, he immediately set out to fashion the ring with all the secret knowledge he had of his craft. He forged it out of a pure and precious stone, which shone with bright colours of shimmering pinks, hues of grey and a hint of brown, and made it spiral into seven loops – resembling the token of the dream in every form imaginable.

Upon its completion, the jeweller took the ring and swiftly set out to the palace. There, he presented the token to the king. "This ring belongs to the young and handsome god of infinite time, Saturn the timekeeper himself," the jeweller promoted. But suspicious of the legend, the keen king told the jeweller that he shall give the jeweller a great fortune if only he would keep the ring and bear it safely. If the young and beautiful god of time should ever come back to collect his token, the king thought the timekeeper would be more merciful towards a guarding ring bearer than a boastful king. And so it was, the jeweller set back home delightfully, where he kept guard over the ring and shared his fortune with his family joyfully.

A few days later, the king was curious to know whether the timekeeper had come to collect his collar or not. And so, he sent one of his knights to pay the jeweller a visit. The knight, however, returned from the jeweller's farm as quickly as he had gone. He bore grave news of the jeweller and his family, for they have been murdered and the ring stolen. But the keen king said to him: "*Thief!* How do you know that the ring had been *stolen* and not *taken?*" To serve justice, he took the knight's title away from him and made the now-former knight wear the ring around his neck for if the timekeeper would ever come to collect his token, he should know what the former knight had done. And so it was that the jeweller had paid with his blood for the ring.

The timekeeper soon learned of this great tragedy when the jeweller and his family entered through paradise's gates. He thought it well to save them and so he turned back time. The jeweller then gave the god of infinite time his ring, for as it turned out, the jeweller's dream – he had once had – was a sign from the young and handsome god of time himself. In return for his good deed, the timekeeper rewarded the jeweller and his family with a fair and prosperous life.

As things stood, the young god had met a betrothed – a fair and young maiden. But she was dying; she had been poisoned by two strange terrors of the night—they were Time the limited and Fear themselves. And moments after this tragic event, Saturn the young and handsome god of infinite time had summoned his seven most trusted prophets, who were also dear friends of his. They had prophesied a great and prosperous prophecy:

"By the band of a marriage forged in the great candle of hope by the hand of faith will become of them, one: idea and passion's fusion. There the token shall bare of secret knowledge, to separate good of evil, and dreamt life, to separate life from death." But the prophesy held a grave warning too: "Be cautious," the prophets said, "all must be done in love. For in love, this divine must be used, for in the wrong hands, evil and death will prevail and spread like a wild plague overall. As strongly, beauty will search for it, so will its indifference."

Saturn had set out to find a forger of this divine artefact and found the jeweller to make their sole nostrum. So he gave the jeweller a vision to make his rings.

The day of the marriage had then come. But on the marriage day just as the young and handsome god wanted to put the ring on the fair maiden's finger, Time and Fear had snatched it from his grasp before he could and away they ran with it. Thus, stolen yet again. Time the limited and Fear have learned of this manifestation and deemed it an abomination.

There and then the god of time swore a vow that he should set out in time to find his ring. He wouldn't stop until he reclaimed it and ultimately present it to his betrothed.

Legend has it that he is still wandering about in time, searching, looking for a ring of pure and precious stone, which shines with bright colours of shimmering pinks, hues of grey and a hint of brown and spirals into seven loops, to give to his betrothed.

- A LEGEND

A Candle under the Water

Prologue

———

A Change of Season

POV Arné

"WHILE I HAD STILL BEEN lying inside my mother's womb, an extraordinary thing had come to pass after the very first time my heart had ever happened to strike a beat. For immediately after it pulsated again – for the second time – I had already experienced the consciousness of an entire life. And it hadn't yet come to throb for the third time ever since; for within that interval before it could, I was awaiting great expectations.

A. PERIL

Part 1

———

Winter

BOOK I

———

A Dream Foraged

POV Arné exc. 1 & 8

.

Chapter One

Left Remained

"**Y**OU'RE GOING TO HELL, BOY!**"** These were the memorable words that dwelt in the thoughts of Arné's mind. They were like thorns impaled to his side, as they injected a great deal of horror into his life. He shut his eyes, and heard how they echoed in his mind, a great too many times before; and yet upon re-opening them, the diction did not decline. Instead, the sound of these words crescendoed into the optical illusion of flames crawling all over burning wooden floors and climbing up walls as they scorched and melted the skin covering his body, all over again. He never really came to understand why Principal Malin had done all those things to him. After all, he had had a good relationship with him; that was, of course, before Arné told him his secret. His spirit was crushed, his heart shattered. He thought that he could trust Principal Malin with this minute detail from the essence of his soul. But he was wrong. Principal Malin, soon after Arné had told him his secret, released all hell upon his being.

It was then, at this period in his life, where Arné found the recurrence of this indwelling memorial, in its present reappearance, somewhat ironic: until this day, he was neither capable of getting it out of his head, nor to process it mentally. As a result, he was often forced to endure the grim sensation again. All the pain. All the suffering it had induced in him. Time after time again. Just like he was forced to tolerate it yet still, tonight.

Externally though, his surroundings portrayed that of a lesser heartache. As it was, the three-story Victorian-style country house, in which he and Saturn had ended-up living in, was filled with diversion. The manor house was situated just outside a small coastal town (which I'll refer to as Old Town for the purpose of this novel). Though the house had once represented a state of resentment, it had become a perfect location for recreation. This made it ideal for that evening's event: Arné's eightieth birthday celebration.

Arné diligently approached the stairs leading up, as he listened to the amusement of their guests coming from the drawing-room, just next door from where he was standing. He closed his eyes.

"You're going to hell, boy," the words echoed sharply through his soul once more.

This was merely one of the motives for his absence. Additionally, he, at that moment, had something more substantial to concern himself with; a valedictory errand to run for aspiration.

He took the first step going up. His one hand grabbed onto the bannister, the other supported him against his cane. He carefully clutched his journal under the armpit of the latter side and ascended more. With every step he took from there on out, he pressed those memories deeper and deeper into his thoughts, just like his feet pressed against the creaking wooden steps beneath them. Upon reaching the first floor, he turned to his right and a few steps farther, he pushed open the doors leading into his study.

By its sudden and robust effect, Arné was struck first by the moonlight, which shone in from an open hanging curtain. It displayed a window-door leading out onto a balcony. The light furnished the room with a meditative mood, as the notable scene charmed his eyes and lured him to his desk right in front of it. To his left, a piano rested in front of a fireplace. It tempted him to smoke a cigarette inside for a moment, so he could blame the fumes on the burning wood. Saturn never liked it when he dragged on inside. Therefore, cautious of the consequences, he decided against it. Instead, he laid his journal down on his desk, switched on the desk-lamp, gazed into the light reflecting off a cherished artefact lying still beside the lamp, and walked away.

Outside a gentle breeze, which carried the scent of saltwater nearby, wavered over his face. He relaxed as he lit-up his cigarette and gazed over the landscape. It felt like serenity. The moon was big and bright, and all the stars glittered next to it like light would reflect off diamonds. A big tree stood fast in the middle of the lawn; it facilitated the charming landscape to paint the forefront of lavender fields and a background with a lake surrounded by a mountain and some hills. It reminded him of a self-written poem he had once recited whenever he had gotten the opportunity to do so:

Let's set forth to the great green hills, my love.

Let's set forth whence the mountain greets the sky
And cries the lake beneath dawn's lonely eye.
Let's set forth thence to be for our behove.

But the winds had always come after the chant to turn on him though. So many times, over. And just like they had come before, they came yet again tonight in a more sensible manner. High clouds overhead started to assemble, and before Arné knew it, rain began to pour down. It was enough to make him go back inside to finish his cigarette. Once inside, he lit the fire and assumed that Saturn will not catch up on the smell.

It is time, he told himself as he threw the cigarette filter into the fire.

But before he went to sit behind his desk, he poured himself a glass of whiskey. He took a sip as he laid back onto his chair. The dry sensation of whisky on his tongue stimulated his tastebuds that eased his line of thought as he put the glass down. He was ready. His hands reached over to take a sheet of letter paper, and as he did, his eyes glanced towards his journal. He looked at it like he would have looked at a good old friend to whom he had to say goodbye, though there was no use for it anymore. That was of course, unlike the letter he was about to compose. Yet, he felt a sense of gloom coming over him too: the letter stood for a closing segment of his life; a conclusion of a noble cause he had once fought for in obstinance. He laid the letter paper down in front of him and picked up his pen. Then, he addressed the letter that shall alter and modify the development of his entire being forever to the love of his life:

Dear Saturn Love,

*May, in hope, this finds you well, my love; wherever
you might wander about in time.*

He paused for a moment, contemplating about the artefact lying next to the lamp and his journal, again. It inspired him to endure. He continued. And while he formulated the letter with all the thoughts that entered his mind, he occasionally took a sip of his whiskey. Letter for letter; word for word; sentence for sentence – he fashioned it. And just before he concluded his message, he drew an envelope, along with the artefact resting still next to the lamp, closer.

Yours forever truly,
Arné Virtue
I love you.

P.S. I'm looking for you.

The letter threw him into a deep trance of reverie; to such an extent, that he had totally lost track of time. It quickly came to an end, though, as he heard footsteps coming up the staircase.

"Arné?"

He threw the letter and the artefact into the envelope.

"Arné, my love!" The voice became louder.

He drank the last sip of whiskey and put the glass down.

"Where are you?" the voice approached the study.

He closed the seal flap with his seal.

Saturn entered the room. "Oh! Here you are, my love."

Arné's heart pounded him to his feet. He was rushed, though that was only partially the reason for his pulsation; the other motive came from a vision of the person standing right in front of him. And for only a split second his imagination had drifted off again. He saw a young and vivacious Saturn carrying his hand into the golden light of day; partially created by the sun, partially created by a smile. The wind whisked Saturn's hair back into honey-golden locks, and the bright blue sky within those same two eyes seduced his fixed gaze upon nothing else at all.

"Arné?" Saturn called.

Arné came back to his senses, as he heard Saturn's voice calling out to him again; and as he did, moonlight replaced that of the sun, and Saturn's hair colour turned back to grey, though those eyes remained transfixed.

He tried to raise a smile, but being too emotionally exhausted after the letter, he failed. "Hi, my love," he said.

Saturn looked at him with prudence. "What were you doing?"

"Writing," he replied as he peered down, and his eyes moved towards the letter.

"Writing. But darling, it's your birthday. Why would you come up to do some writing when we're all downstairs celebrating?" asked Saturn. "Is everything okay?"

"Yeah-no, everything's fine," he said. "I'm sorry, I don't know what I was thinking." He stepped from behind his desk and started to walk towards Saturn.

"Well, was it something important?" Saturn asked concerningly.

"You could say so, yes."

"What was it about then?"

"A letter…" he tried to explain, but he couldn't find enough words to do so.

"A letter," Saturn said and then repeated thoughtfully, "a letter?"

"Yes," he said. "A letter." He turned around as he referred to it. But it was no longer there on the desk where he just left it to be. It seemed to have vanished into mid-air. And just as he turned back to face Saturn, confused as he was about what he just witnessed, his eyes could not believe what they saw. It worked: there in front of him, Saturn stood with the envelope in hand. Opened.

"You mean—" said Saturn.

"Yes," Arné said, still with a sense of disbelief.

"I got your letter!" cried Saturn.

Chapter Two

A Search for Belonging

IT ALMOST FEELS LIKE A lifetime – an existence – had passed after I tried to give Saturn a letter; though, in reality, it had only been around ten years since that distinct day. It was supposed to have been a message of hope that I had once thought a deliverance to exchange. An adjustment, forever, regarding the direction of my being. And I often reflected on it; imagining what would have befallen my part if only those words had triumphed into Saturn's sight. Though I was sure of it; Saturn would have known then that I was searching. I'd have to lie if I said that I haven't fantasised about the rest ever: the counter remnant - the denouement of our story - which remained a mystery to my daily thoughts that entered my conscious mind. But this was not the case.

As it was, I was twenty-five now, and things have changed since then. The scenery. The physiques. The day-to-day existence. I suppose this is what life is like. It is good, in a way, I guess – the change. I couldn't help but feel a kind of oppression coming over me too. Whenever I *did* think about it: the experiences of farewells to the mattering elements of our lives. It occurs time-and-time over again. We see new places, and we meet new people, and we act upon new duties. Don't get me wrong; I find these exciting – but I couldn't let Saturn go. Saturn was, and always will be, that one piece that lacked for the fulfilment of my puzzle; the element of my account, I would never have sworn to leave out; a person I required, just simply needed in my life.

I was reminiscing about these developments of one's life one day on my midday walk, as I roamed the city streets (which I shall refer to as New City for the purpose of this novel). The water underneath the bridges reflected the sunlight of a beautiful day, and clearly flowed along the canals like leaves would dance with the autumn wind. The city appeared renewed as I walked the allays in between the taxpayer-buildings of the centre.

I had moved here from a small coastal town (called Old Town) when I was fifteen. It wasn't my choice, and I haven't seen the skyline of another ever since. Although I didn't necessarily admire the city-life, this was where I desired to be – not merely for any other purpose than Saturn. That goes without saying that I had my occupation.

Henceforth, excursions were reserved for the latter. But I did have one good friend, called Joy (whom I met one evening in the suburbs of the city) with whom I would've met up with at least thrice weekly for either an evening beer or lunch (whichever would fancy us most that day). This would exclude the occasional visit to the other's house).

Nevertheless, I was doing some window-shopping among the taxpayer-buildings when something in one of the clothing stores caught my attention. *Saturn*, I ruminated to myself as I stared through one of the displaying windows of the store. *How, among the 300 000 inhabitants residing in the city, did I spot Saturn?* I was amazed, to say the least. It only occurred once before (a day I often did but never yearned to recall), and never had I ever re-encountered Saturn again without looking. This was the second time.

I went in and pretended to do some browsing myself. I followed Saturn on the opposite side of one of the clothing racks, figuring out how I should approach this. Abruptly our eyes connected from the quick glances we shared at each other.

I smiled. "Hi." I didn't know what else to say.

Saturn grinned awkwardly. "Hi."

I craved for the persistence of our encounter, a development from a greeting into a conversation. And without knowing what else to do, I swiftly swung around the rack and uttered the very first words that pierced through my mind. "That will look good on you," I said (it was an orange button-up shirt riddled with coconut trees).

"Thanks," Saturn said, holding the shirt up, and raised an eyebrow. "But I think that I'm more than capable of picking out my own clothes." Saturn then put the shirt back on the rack and started to walk away.

"I'll buy it for you," I said. I couldn't let this opportunity slip from my grasp.

"No," Saturn said to me, glancing back in motion. "You won't." grinned Saturn.

I quickly went over to the rack and picked up the shirt. "As a gift," I said. "So, you can't say no."

Saturn turned around and simpered. "Okay," said Saturn. "And then what?"

21

"Maybe then, you could wear it on our first date?"

Saturn laughed. "No," Saturn said and turned back around.

"Come on," I said, desperately.

Saturn turned around again. "So, it's going to be from shirt to date, uh?"

"Well, yeah. I mean – is there something wrong with that?"

"No. Not in the slightest," said Saturn. "I just thought that you would have been able to do a little bit better than that. Besides, I don't even know you. And what makes you think that I would like to go on a date with you?"

"Oh, come on. Where else should I have been able to see you and ask you out on a date? Plus, I know for sure that you would have asked me to go away by now if you didn't have some sort of interest in me."

Saturn smiled. "That's a good point. But still – I don't know you."

I walked over to Saturn and held my hand out. "My name is Arné," I said.

Saturn grinned and took my hand. "Mine is Saturn, it is nice to meet you, Arné."

"Likewise," I said. "So, what do you say? You can find out the rest tonight – by the by isn't this how people meet and get to know each other?" I grinned and put the shirt back. "So, at seven then. There's a small café-restaurant just across the street."

Saturn smirked and walked past me. "I thought you're going to buy me that shirt?" Saturn whispered into my ear.

"So, it's a yes then?"

"It is an I'll see," Saturn said and walked away towards the checkout.

I quickly followed. And after I bought the shirt, we said goodbye as I handed it over.

The rest of the day dragged on sluggishly. Though, how it always feels in peerless anticipation. As a result, I arrived at the café at least an hour early, after I groomed myself for the evening (which took me roughly the remainder of the day's hours). I waited outside the café-restaurant just across the street from where Saturn and I had met moments before. In desperation to fill the hour and make it pass quicker, I must have smoked at least three cigarettes, which, when I think about it now, I shouldn't have done, as Saturn loathes the reek of it. At about quarter to seven, I went in to get us an available table. It didn't take me long, and it gave me just enough time to go out and drag out one last smoke (I didn't think about the consequences either then).

I took a pull from the cigarette when, out of nowhere, I felt someone poking my shoulder. I turned around.

"Hi," said Saturn.

Exhaling the smoke shyly to my hip, I greeted back. I desperately wanted the vapour to go towards the other side, but the wind decided it would be perfect if it goes directly into Saturn's face. "You're wearing that shirt!" I said.

"Yeah," Saturn said sarcastically. "And you smoke?"

"Recreational thing," I said rather awkwardly. "But you. Look at you. You look amazingly beautiful," I said, trying to divert our conversation away from my unfortunate habit.

Saturn laughed. "It looks awful, thank you very much," Saturn said sarcastically, which I loved. "You owe me breakfast for this one."

"It's a second date then," I said. "But I still think that it looks lovely."

"Yeah, well, you'll be the only one here who does. I can promise you that. And we'll have to see about that second date after tonight."

And we did see to it; after our pleasant evening spent together, Saturn accepted my invitation to breakfast. After breakfast, we saw each other again for lunch in one of the city's parks.

It was around midday that day when Saturn's figure approached me from the distance as I waited near the park's entrance. My lips beaming by the rise of the appearance, and my gaze never veered from it. I was astounded to see how well this was going. My pounding heart made me feel alive.

"Thanks again for meeting up here," Saturn greeted me with a hug.

"Yeah, no problem."

It was close enough from Saturn's work to have slipped away for only a couple of minutes.

"So, what do you do again?" I already knew the answer.

"Oh, I'm a music teacher at the University of Performance Arts. Just there. That building over there." Saturn pointed at a modern building on the other side of the park from where we were standing. "Do you see it?"

"Hard to miss," I grinned, barely even concentrating on the building.

We continued gallivanting along the walkways of the park, relishing in our conversation. We found pleasure in each other's jokes and clicked on more philosophical and severe matters related to our metaphysical wisdom (something firmly established in both our lives). The trail led us alongside calming streams, flourishing trees, blossoming flowers, that eventually led us to a kiosk in the centre of the park where we ordered ourselves two colas and sandwiches. I offered to pay. And after I had done so, I took the meals from the countertop.

"Here you go," I said as I turned around, expecting to give one of the meals to Saturn.

But as I had done so, I was unexpectedly answered by a line of frowned upon expressions. Their eyes and faces elucidated which I found evident after a second: Saturn had vanished; though as if into mid-air. Opposing the physiques, it didn't come to me as much as a deadened shock. I mean, I didn't believe that it would last long, considering how – under the particular circumstances – we had engaged the day before.

Chapter Three

Time

I OFTEN MEDITATED ON THE philosophy of other people's memoirs and what they mirrored. I would then admire them in such a way that I'd wonder if mine were, in any way, profoundly different from theirs. They always seemed so much more fortunate than I was, and it made me consider them only abler at hiding their afflictions. I never took happiness and joy for granted. When and if I found it, I tried to keep my grip on it for as long as possible. But it always appeared to have slipped from my grasp.

Saturn's disappearances the offset case: fix and loose. And since, I still connected everything to Saturn: my happiness, joy, love, time, life, everything really. I told myself that if only I could find Saturn actually, then everything will improve. Everything will fall into place. But still, it never occurred. I can always remember the first time I felt that sensation, though as if I had memorised it. And although it feels like a long time since that day, it only happened when I was twenty-one.

As it was, we bumped into each other one rainy evening outside one of the movie theatres a couple of blocks from the city centre. The clouds blinded the moon as the rainfall difficilitated the recognition of one's vicinity, whereas the city-lights clarified one's most adjacent street-signs and buildings. Trying to keep dry, I was running from whatever shelter I could find to another, when out of nowhere, through the mist of the rain, the appearance struck me like a spotlight; the contemplation of Saturn's face was a flash of great revelation. Like if everything was going to be okay. But it was accompanied soon after with the exact binary of opposition—a recession.

"Saturn?" I recalled saying with astonished disbelief.

Saturn was laughing under a shared umbrella with a friend when my voice halted them near my side.

"It's me, Arné."

The blank expression on Saturn's face communicated adversity.

"Don't you remember? Arné, from the orphanage?"

"Sorry, but I think you must have me confused with someone else."

"You don't remember?"

"I'm really sorry. But I don't know who you are. I'm sorry," Saturn repeated politely and continued walking on with the friend. It was a repetition that aided in the memorisation of the accident.

As it turned out, Saturn had amnesia; something I had only discovered later after Saturn had told me all about it. As it was, Saturn's backstory would always stay the same, with some variations to it here and there: "When I was eight years old, I had lost both my parents. My brother and I were sent to live in an orphanage house remotely from here. When I was fifteen years old, I had hit my head extremely hard, and the next thing I could remember was waking up in a hospital. After I had recovered, I lived with a woman named Hope and today, I'm living with my brother, Jupiter, his wife, and their child. And I am a music teacher too."

Nevertheless, still till that present day, the amnesia was something I associated with the letter; the incident was a declaration of my message's unsuccessful deliverance. A hope lost. For, if only it had reached Saturn's hand in time, Saturn would have known then that I was coming. Searching. The amnesia would have been a mere pawn easily overthrown. It wasn't long after that day – after either the amnesia or the disappearances would have prevented our tryst a couple of times over – that I had realised, I will have to seek Saturn until the day we both found each other actually. It left me to make Saturn fall in love with me all over again, each and every time. I haven't stopped ever since. And I'm sure that this would not have been the requirement, had our lives turned out differently; and although I thought about it time after time again, I couldn't avert the feeling of euphoria waning, every time Saturn had vanished with it. And yet, till this day, whenever it did transpire, blood still drained from my face, and adrenaline would again rake through my veins, just like that very first day.

It had been a week today since Saturn's last disappearance. It left me too timid to set a foot outside, and my emotions chained me to my apartment; it assigned me to live off anything appropriate I could possibly discover in my cupboard and refrigerator. And although I didn't think it healthy, in any way, this was normal. This was how long it usually took me to get over the last time Saturn would have disappeared. And whenever I did finally build up enough courage to go outside, either by myself or by Joy's aid, I would generally go to that place I last saw Saturn.

It was in this way that I found myself entering a bar a few blocks away from my own apartment. Its proximity had me walking instead of driving. The bar wasn't something fancy or out of the ordinary. All the necessities were included: a bar counter, with its sad-drunk; a couple of booths, with colleagues or friends, either joking around or complaining; one pool table, utilised by some fellow trying to show off his skills to either his buddies or a girl; a stage, occasionally employed by a couple of jazz performers; and a dance floor, occupied only if the music wasn't too bad.

Joy was sitting at the bar alone, talking to the bartender, when I had entered. Grace, his girlfriend, who I also knew on a more personal level, would sometimes accompany us, but lately, she's been missing due to some emotional problems. Joy's light-dark skin, green-eyes, dark hair, and chivalry earned him grand status as a quite eligible bachelor. And if it wasn't for Grace and his own loyalty, I'm sure he would have been able to pick up just about anyone in the bar he fancied. It still caught me by surprise, though, every time I saw him that way. He hasn't always been this sociable person who could build a conversation with just about anyone he aspired to; there was a time he was too intimidated to set his foot outside, not even mentioning places like this one.

Joy glanced to the entrance as he saw me enter. He greeted the bartender with a gentle slap on the bar and what looked like him ordering us each a beer before he came over to greet me. "Hey, Arné, buddy," he said as he gave me a brotherly hug. "It feels like it's been weeks. Or maybe—" Joy laughed sarcastically, "it's because it's been weeks."

I returned a grin. "Always," I sighed and rolled my eyes.

"That's okay," he said and put his arm around me. "I ordered us each a beer," he continued and led us to an open booth where we undressed our coats and sat across from one another.

Our conversation took us down many roads travelling from our personal lives to our professional ones. This was the norm for our exchanges, considering the number of times we saw each other. Joy was studying to become a doctor, and I had the impression that we would see less of each other now that he is graduating this year and will start with his internship and residency training soon. And I'm sure that if it isn't his work that will take his time, it most certainly will be time spent with Grace (as I suppose we all would prioritise). However, our lack of convergence for weeks induced a parley of a more profound heartfelt matter: Saturn, myself and everything which had transpired in the interim.

Joy signalled for the second round of beers. "I don't know why you can't just find someone else, bro?"

It was, in fact, a good question. I didn't know either. And with everything that had happened thus far, I couldn't see why it would matter now anymore. But then, just as I would consider it, one question would come to mind – the same one that always did whenever I deemed such a thought. "Do you think that it's possible to go to the future to change the past?" I asked disregarding his own.

Joy remained silent for a moment, and I could see that he was confused. "Good question," he said. "And under your peculiar circumstance, a perfect one indeed," he added. "Why do you want to know?"

"Just a thought," I said.

A sociable waitress came to give us our beers. We joked around for a second before she went to tend to other tables.

"Does it have something to do with Saturn?" The conversation turned back, seriously.

"In a way," I said. "But still just a thought." I didn't want to talk too much about it. It would have raised other tough questions I didn't aspire to have asked.

"Well," Joy said. "You can talk to me about it once it's all straightened out then."

"Will do," I grinned.

With our half-finished beers on the table, Joy glanced at his wristwatch. "Oh shoot," he said. "I've got to get home. See how Grace's doing. Probably sleeping, but I just want to make sure she's fine. And then there's work tomorrow morning too," he added.

We dressed our coats as we stood up, leaving our beers behind, and went to pay our bill.

"Did you drive?" Joy asked as we came out of the bar.

"Walked," I said. "And you?"

"Took a cab. Couldn't find the keys of the car and didn't want to bother Grace." He laughed. He was rather forgetful for someone who was studying to become a doctor. But then again, I guess it was what made him, him. "Want to take one with me?"

"Sure, why not." It was late, and I didn't feel like walking anyway.

He signalled for a taxicab, and we took the first one that pulled over. Once inside, I offered the cab to drop him off first, although Joy lived remotely from the inner city. We didn't say much in the car, except when it pulled over at Joy's suburban house.

The house had me nostalgic as I glanced over it. I could still remember playing in that same house's backyard with a beautiful voice calling my name. As it was, this was the house where I had grown up in. I had decided to consign it to Joy and Grace a few months ago, as their relationship appeared to become extremely serious, and I wanted them to have someplace private, which they could call their own.

"Keep care," Joy greeted as he opened the passenger door.

"Will do. And you too," I greeted. "Send my love to Grace," I added as Joy closed the cab's passenger door.

I went straight back home myself.

The following day I found myself in the park where I last saw Saturn. It was a beautiful sunny day, and as it had rained that morning, the florae of the park were ever greener. I listened to children laughing, and I watched lovers – old and young – holding hands as I had passed them while I was walking the walkways of the park and carrying my journal lightly with me in my left hand. An hour had flown by since I arrived. Saturn was nowhere to be seen; thus, I quickly decided to give up on the park, but I wanted to rest my feet for a while before I left. I found a bench near one of the ponds in the centre of the park, and there I sat down, placed my journal to my left, and lit myself a cigarette.

The duckpond was not something out of the ordinary, but I found it fascinating. An island was centred right in the middle of the pond where birds and other waterfowl had their nests. My eyes were feasted on them as I watched them fly to and fro and going about their habits;

I found it both enthralling and calming in a way that they carried away all my cares in the world with them. Nature has always had this effect on me – I remember when I was younger, I would make up just about any excuse to set my feet outside, no matter how important the errand was I had to run. It helped me to process my line of thoughts. The pond and the fowls were mesmerising; and completely forgetting about my cigarette, I started to muse upon my life:

I vividly remembered opening my eyes to a sight so unfamiliar, that even significance had no meaning. And although I couldn't find the words to describe any of it at the time, I remembered a middle-aged woman, with tanned skin mixed with a tint of gold, and topaz eyes shining bright like the sun on a warm summer's day, gaping at me. It was only sometime after that day, I came to understand why: because the boy who sat right in front of her had just wet his pants; and though age and its accordance did not have much meaning to me then, but as it was, I had met her when I was fifteen.

She was a magnificent woman, Miss Precious, as she was called. She was tall and robust and would always carry herself with dignity and accordance wherever she went. I could still remember till this day how she introduced herself to me (probably because she had to do it a couple of times over).

"My name is Miss Precious," she said and would always speak with an air of blissfulness and forgiveness. "And I will be your foster parent until we find you a more permanent solution."

But that solution had never come, I had ended up staying with her. And yet, as I think back onto it now when I had found her, I had attained a beacon that could guide me someplace where I belonged: she was the essence of something I had – at one point in my life – only dreamed of having or hoped for from another. Therefore, her image was ungraspable; and yet right in front of me, her existence was as clear as daylight.

The months which followed that day had come to be some of the most critical months of my entire life. Miss Precious had taught me everything I needed to know about accordance with primary conduct and lifestyle.

"Bathroom," she'd say and then she'd go on and teach me how to use it.

I would repeat it.

"We eat with a fork and a knife and a spoon, and this is a plate and a glass and a mug," she'd say and then she'd go on and teach me how to use each of the individual objects.

I would repeat it.

Then she would let me go outside of her suburban house to play with her pet-dog and let me watch how it went about its own business.

"Dog," she'd say.

And I would repeat.

"Look how he plays with his ball," she'd say. "The silly old goose." She laughed.

And I would laugh with her.

We would then have continued by playing, ourselves.

"I throw the ball," she'd say.

And I would repeat what she had said and pursued by pitching the ball back.

Sentences got more challenging as time advanced, and concepts became more familiar to me. And although this was all sound, it would only be some time after those days, that I'd seen, language and concepts were the least important, for the most essential thing Miss Precious could possibly have taught me, was love. When I think back to all those years ago, I must admit; still, I could never find anybody who could make me feel loved the way she did. And it made me wonder what love truly is.

By the age of sixteen, I have learned a lot of things. And although they carried a great deal of importance still, primary conduct and lifestyle were something in my past; it wasn't pivotal to my life anymore, for I had started with primary education, home-schooled by Miss Precious herself. The expansion of my language skills allowed me to see further; I began to grasp complex and complicated ideas of and about things. My cognitive understanding allowed me to see deeper into the meaning of life. My ability to have a conversation with someone else had inaugurated, and it ultimately opened new doors for me.

Therefore, by the time I had turned seventeen, I had started to have therapy sessions with Miss Precious herself – subsequently, discovering her profession. My life was instead a mystery to both Miss Precious and myself. It all seemed so discreet. Yet even I didn't know what secrets my mind had concealed from myself. I couldn't recall anything before that day I first coincided with Miss Precious. And although I had trusted her with my entire life, I couldn't help but sense a feeling of distrust from her side – projected from my own insecurities. However, I knew she would never have blamed me for any such impression; instead, she would have held the people, who were commanding my life before, accountable. But still, I wouldn't have accused her of this type of suspicion after all that was. That was one of the reasons why I had agreed on therapy. Anything really, to help me retain and learn about my past, and for Miss Precious to rest reassured. And I did. I had learned something within that year. Something vital to the importance of my existence. The disclosure had revealed itself to me one afternoon, following one of my sessions with Miss Precious.

"Good progress," Miss Precious said as she opened the door leading out of her bureau.

The appearance of an alarmed woman (not much older than Miss Precious) struck us both as we stepped from the room. She was dressed, in an overcoat too big for her, and her black hair looked unkempt.

"Precious?" the woman said tremblingly.

"Yes," Miss Precious said as she walked over to the woman.

"Is everything alright? Can I do something for you?"

"Only a quick word." The woman regarded me in-depth, as Miss Precious stepped between us.

"Of course. Let's go inside shall we."

They went inside, and the door that had been left ajar tempted me to eavesdrop on their conversation. The woman was whispering, unlike Miss Precious, who spoke in an authoritative tone.

"Is the boy, okay?" the woman asked concerningly.

"Yes. The boy is fine. What had happened to him?" asked Miss Precious.

"There had been a murder and a robbery," the woman said.

"I cannot speak much of it, please understand, it's too dreadful to think about it. Except that… I can say—"

"What?"

"A child had died," the woman said frightfully. "Please tell me, is the boy safe now with you?"

"I can assure you that he is in good hands."

"Good," the woman said and swiftly disappeared from the bureau.

And that was it. Miss Precious never articulated anything of its record to me, and I never mentioned my intrusion of that intimate matter to her. And though I didn't know who it was at that time, it wasn't the last time I ever saw the woman; although I did not know, what the purpose of their rally was all about, I would soon come to learn more of it. Nevertheless, that conversation was engraved in my mind, and I had not come to let go of it ever since; not for one single moment for the remainder of my entire life.

I turned eighteen soon after that day. Miss Precious had continued to teach me, and I had a therapy session once a week. And although nothing had changed much, I could remember that I had started to experience an abnormal progression of dreams. Images so vivid that they had appeared as memories to my imagination. Visions of my past. Sometimes they were long, though as if I had lived in that dream-world for weeks – other times only hours – yet awakening from them assuming I had the typical seven-to-nine-hour sleep I frequently would have had. They had seemed related to my younger years, though as if they were distant memories from my past. Almost like I remembered what had happened to me through my dreams. But nothing much had come from it really, except for a few discussions about them with Miss Precious in therapy; when she would ask me where I was, or what I had done.

"I was four last night," I would simply have answered, "and I was in an orphanage house. I think I was there for one month – I had my birthday." Always an orphanage house, though my age and the duration of the time spent there would have changed.

In the year I had turned nineteen, my presentation portrayed that of any other young man my age. It was therefore an ideal time for me to start with a new therapy line, as Miss Precious had counselled. She usually continued with the type of treatment with some of her more challenging patients. It was called hypnotherapy. She would put me in a trance to ascertain more grounds concerning my past. I, myself, was eager to become more knowledgeable over the matter; I envied a history. Any risks were merely boundaries I desired to reverse. I'd done anything to uncover and reconstruct unspecified derangements. Albeit my mind had relinquished any of the nitty-gritty things of hypnotherapy, it did keep safeguard over the disclosures my mind had confessed. Affirmingly, every brief encounter facilitated Miss Precious to break the code leading to my subconsciousness. However, it wasn't until a few weeks had passed when we had a significant breakthrough. The day's session commenced like any other. I entered, Miss Precious and I had a brief discussion about my feelings, including other personal matters such as a lovely new experience I might have had or some ordeal I have encountered. Then, we continued with hypnotherapy.

"Close your eyes, Arné," Miss Precious said, as she would always do at the derivation.

I would always strive to do my best of what she asked of me.

She would then put on a metronome. "I would like you to breathe in— and out— deep. In— and out—" Then she would come closer to me. She'd take my hand and start tapping in my palm. "I want you to listen to the sound of my voice and relax. Clear your mind. Breathe in— and out— deeply, in— and out—" She'd always tell me these calming words and ask me to breathe throughout the sessions.

I remember that day becoming slumberous, though as if I went from one world to another: to a more dreamlike one.

"I want you to go back to the very first day of your life," she said calmingly and remained silent for a moment. "Tell me, what do you see?"

"I see nothing. My eyes are closed. But I feel naked, and I'm wet. My heart is beating."

"G—"

"Now I see you," I abruptly announced.

"Where are you?" Miss Precious asked, and I remembered the sound of her voice breaking through as if she was perplexed and anxious.

"In this room," I said.

It didn't make any sense. Not to me, neither to Miss Precious I assumed. Still, why did I see Miss Precious? Why was I in this room? I was bewildered by it all, I suppose Miss Precious as much as I was. But she had persisted calmly within the clutter.

"Good," she said. "I want you to go to the day you were born," she said and once again remained silent for a moment. "Tell me, what do you see?"

"Nothing," I said. I couldn't see anything, though as if I had never been born.

"And the day after that?"

"I see a room filled with doctors and nurses. They are wearing doctors' clothes. They pick me up. They smile. They feed me. They give me toys. I feel warm."

"Good," she said. "I want you to come back to reality."

I opened my eyes. Miss Precious was smiling.

Similarly, like I had opened my eyes there in Miss Precious's bureau, I came to open my eyes back in the park where I drifted off while contemplating the duckpond and forgetting about my cigarette. A quick-moving shadow had passed me; it had drawn me back to the present. I glanced at my hand. My cigarette was burned out. Then I turned my head to see who the shadow represented, and as I did, my eyes swelled.

Saturn, I thought. Saturn looked benign as always. The calm barefooted spirit put a smile on my face.

"Oh! Sorry," said Saturn. "I hope that I didn't— I didn't mean to startle you there."

I grinned. Saturn proceeded by sitting on the bench next to mine and placing a bag on the seat.

"No, no, no! Not at all," I said, throwing the cigarette butt into the dustbin next to my bench. Saturn took some breadcrumbs from the bag and smiled. "Do you want some?"

"No, I'm good." I simpered. "I just ate something, so I'm stuffed."

Saturn laughed. "Not for you," Saturn said. "It's for the ducks."

I laughed as I looked towards the island and then back to Saturn. "Oh— Yeah— sure. Why not?" I said and took a handful of the crumbs.

We exchanged pleasantries, and after a friendly conversation about life and experiences (some jokes included), we decided to exchange phone numbers. Eventually, we went our separate ways.

When that evening came, aching to call Saturn up for a rendezvous the following day, I ventured to convince myself of other things: the number was just lost, the phone was only off; but as it was, I dialled a non-existing number.

Chapter Four

Time After Time

I HAD COME TO THINK of it as an invariant: that things will forever stay the same. As though, I would have attained what I had sought for, it would have been purloined from me, always; Fleeting – tirelessly distancing itself from me. Yet, I couldn't help myself but stay the course. As it resembled, my life, the equal of binary oppositions: euphoria and depression, discovery, and privation; for, every time it would have repeated itself permanently.

That being said, at the inception of my quest – euphoria and innovation – I would have found Saturn, and my senses would have bequeathed me. This time Saturn will stay, I would tell myself. Saturn will not disappear. Not this time around.

In its midst, the latter would have seemed like it; the illusion would have deceived me to such an extent that I would have become to believe in it. And how could I refuse it? Every time, it portrayed itself as an opportunity. We would go on a date, a second if I were so lucky. But if I were to be truly fortunate enough, we would have had weeks together, sometimes even months. But that was not always the case.

At the exodus of my quest – depression and privation – Saturn would have evaporated into thin air. A farewell without the greet. I'd then recognise its disguise. And although the disappearances would have facilitated the subsequent chance of appeal (for Saturn wouldn't always have considered going out with me too, and it resulted in the conflict's oblivion), I couldn't help myself but to come and denounce them.

I looked for three days, roaming the streets of the city, when I finally spotted Saturn again, entering a coffee shop. I quickly followed. Saturn was sitting at a booth not far from the doors where I had just come through. I ordered myself a coffee and went over to make an introduction.

"May I sit with you?" I said as I approached Saturn's table. "Everywhere else is full." And fortunately, it was.

Saturn looked around. "Of course."

"I'm Arné, by the way," I said as I placed my journal on the table.

"I'm Saturn."

We exchanged pleasantries before the waitress called for our coffees, and we proceeded to drink them while having a lovely not-too-long conversation that gave me just enough time to ask Saturn out again that evening. Saturn accepted my invitation before having gone back to work soon after that.

We had a lovely evening at a seafood restaurant, and the day after that we spent some time together roaming the streets of the city, doing some window shopping. But there wasn't any third time, though. Saturn had disappeared again.

The departure had me fixed to my bed the morning after that day. In a search for a sense of reconciliation, I stared out of my open bedroom window, observing the curtains next to it dance with the wind and sunlight entering the room. My thoughts ran wild, but my attention was quickly substituted by the reverie of the accident that had given rise to my peculiar circumstance:

I retained the first time I had travelled in time by my own accord; as it was, I had done so before, unconsciously. Though, I had not come to know of it until I had taken control over the ability myself. It all inaugurated in the evening I had turned twenty. I remembered lying in bed restlessly and frustrated; not only because I couldn't find a way to put my mind at ease, but also because I had come to hate my birthday. To be frank, I had started to hate age all together with it; it had represented a great misfortune for myself: I didn't have a past, and even if I did, I didn't know anything about it.

Who am I, and where do I come from? I shouted in my head, many times over. It didn't fit. How could I exist, and not even know these fundamental questions about my life? I tried to think harder back and retrieve it. Anything. Anything to navigate me into my amour. A face, a building, a sound. I didn't really care what I would be, as long as it was just something. I just needed to know something. Something I could work with. I suddenly emanated a feeling of drunkenness within my head from all the ferocity I had felt. I clenched my fists and squeezed my eyes. My heart, pounding. And out of nowhere a feeling of light-headedness came over me. I tried to grab hold of my bed; it felt like I was falling right through it. But the bed was no longer there.

Instead, the warmth of my bed covers had been replaced by cold grass beneath my feet. The sun blinded my eyes as I had opened them in eagerness to the sound of children laughing. Confused, and slightly dizzy, I looked around: aback, a big building and in front, children playing on a lawn under a big tree. And then I studied my hands disturbingly for what I saw were the hands of a child. I panicked. I fought for breath.

What is going on? I thought, *what is this?* I squeezed my eyes shut and clenched my fists tighter than before. *Back. Go back,* I thought, *I want to go back.*

And there I was again, under the covers of my bed in Miss Precious's house. A sudden but potent adventure.

"Miss Precious, ma'am!" I roared as I rushed to her room. And then I screeched the one thing I could possibly think of that could have explained this supernatural event: "I have travelled in time!"

She was horrified, to say the least. Not merely because of the news, but though firstly for the commotion that I had made entering her room.

After she was fully awake, she let me sit beside her on the bed, explaining myself and re-informed her of what had arrived.

"Arné," she said wistfully. She was still half asleep. "I'm sure that it was only a nightmare."

I nodded, thinking the opposite of what she had said.

"Come on. I'll make you a nice cup of honey tea to relax, and you can try to fall asleep again."

I didn't blame her for the disbelief. Frankly, I would have behaved the same way if I were her. Nonetheless, it didn't stop me from experimenting.

It took me about a month of travelling back and forth in time, assessing my theory – to be absolutely sure that this was the case; that I could, in fact, wander in time. My scrutiny had allowed me to remark many things during that time. And though there were many, two of those had come to excel.

The first and paramount of these discernings were my subsistent hours. As it was, I had acknowledged this fact when I tried to go back and live my childhood; this being said, the first nine years of my life. I craved to perceive what my childhood was like – to see who raised me. But I was struck by the fact that I could not go back to those years. At first, the matter was confusing; indeed, if I could travel in time, I should be able to go and breathe in that era of my life. Then, I got an idea. A concept that would transmute into the foundation of my knowledge surrounding my ability. I travelled into the unknown future – one day to be precise. Then I came back. And when I wanted to go to that same day again, I couldn't; the verdict – for I had already lived it. So had come the day I noticed that once I had lived a second of my life, I lived it, and can't relive it. With that understanding, I apprehended that the dreams I had once so often experienced were, in fact, not dreams but the actual endurance of my past – which explained the lucidity of them. Hence the disclosure: the first nine years of my life, I had spent at an orphanage, though uncertain of the exact location. And the last thing I could identify befalling me was a matron telling me that I was being relocated because of my age. I had concluded that I was given up at birth. So, before I have known about my gift, I had travelled in time without my informed consent.

The second of those discernings was the creation of timelines; though it was only a thought at the time, I believed my theory adequate. If I go to the past and make some specific modifications, it must surely change my future, resulting in another timeline. Nevertheless, it was only an idea at the time, and it would only be sometime after that day when I had learned of the fact's more grotesque horrors.

After that month, one last thing had remained unclarified: I had to demonstrate to Miss Precious that my report was indeed not false. So had come one evening when we both sat around the dinner table. I was relatively silent that evening, thinking about how I can approach the revealing matter.

"So, how was your day?" asked Miss Precious.

"It was good," I replied straight to the point. I was acting like a real teenager.

"That's nice," she said, slightly not too upset by my approach. "Anything interesting happened?"

This was my chance. She had opened the door for my disclosure. "Well, now that you have asked," I said slightly hesitantly, "there *is* something."

"I see," she said, intrigued by what I had just said. "And?"

I stayed still for a while. "Well," I started, "you remember about a month ago, well, when I woke you."

"Yes," she said reflectively.

"Well, something new has happened."

"Arné," she spoke wistfully, "I thought we put this behind us. I'm sure it was just another nightmare."

"I can prove it to you."

"What do you mean?"

"A Mister Frank will come to see you tomorrow."

Neither of us knew how to respond after that. And what followed was a couple of awkward minutes until Miss Precious decided to say something, again.

"I was looking at some universities you might attend. Maybe we could have a look at it tomorrow morning?" She said calmly within the discomfiture, trying to change the subject.

I was starting to get older, and Miss Precious wanted a promising future for me. She had begun to look at some universities a few weeks ago.

"That'll be nice."

And though Miss Precious was not rebuking, the rest of the evening was played in uncomfortable silence until we both went to bed.

The following morning, while Miss Precious brewed us some breakfast (as she always did) and while I was sitting by the dining table, the front door's bell rang.

"That's odd," she said as she went to see who it was. "I wonder who that could be." Her head turned to gaze upon me, just like she had turned the doorknob to open the door. "Extraordinary," she declared with reclamation. For what she had seen was the revelation of my disclosure – Mr Frank was standing by the door.

He was a former patient of Miss Precious and just wanted to drop by and drop off some sweet biscuits; he was moving away and thought it well to thank Miss Precious for everything she had done.

I can only assume that this type of exposure had raised as many questions as it had answered for her. Nevertheless, Miss Precious was intrigued by the curiosity of the circumstance. She didn't say another word after the man had left. Instead, Miss Precious hastened to her study and abruptly sifted through all her books.

"Arné," she said when she finally approached me, "I want you to take this book," she placed the book in my hand. "There's no obligation, Arné. But I would like you to keep a diary about your life, experiences, day-to-day events, or even simple thoughts."

It was, in fact, nothing like a diary, nor a journal. It was something intended to be a record, a logbook of my being; something to help me keep track of my days and maintain some sense of chronological growth. Miss Precious told me never to let it out of my sight. To carry it with me wherever I might go. And I must admit now, it was a great idea, to say the least; of which I had not bothered myself with, unfortunately; and it would only be some time after she had given me the journal that I would actually have begun writing in it.

I fell asleep while straying off into the recollections of my being. The next thing I remembered was my phone ringing on my nightstand; something that woke me from what felt like a mere quick nap. I reached over. Joy asked me if I were up for a piano recital that night at the City State Opera. We didn't talk long; I agreed, and we both hung up. I was just about to put my phone down when something terrifying caught my attention on the display screen. It was the date. And though I did not find it in any way exceedingly radical, as I had become accustomed to this sort of condition, I was astounded; for the time indicated on the screen attested that I was thirty-one. I still travelled in time without my informed consent; sometimes only because I had already lived the succeeding time. Consequently, I wasn't too bothered by it. Not significantly. Though it did make me less in the mood to go out. But I figured it might do me some good.

And it did, I met Saturn again that evening; I must have known that Saturn went to evenings like such – it never crossed my mind. Nevertheless, there we both were – two souls wandering around, attracted like magnets towards each other; it would make one think that it was meant to be.

And it was, or at least, it was for twelve years: Saturn remained a music teacher as I started to work as a supermarket manager. We got engaged soon after we met, married not long after that, and had two beautiful children together. Saturn Jr. was our eldest boy, and Chris, our youngest daughter. We lived in New City in a suburban house not far from where Joy and Grace and their own child had come to live. Jupiter and his family stayed close by too; though as if we were all neighbours. So had our family grown. Life seemed tolerant. It was congenial and populated, more than I could ever have come to imagine it would be like. And for those twelve years, the impression that Saturn and I shall grow old together consumed me.

And thus, it was that one sombre evening, both inside the house and out, that I sneaked to my study holding my journal fast. It was a perfect evening. I didn't want anybody to notice me – neither Saturn nor the children – they might have had questions. Hence, I placed the journal under my arm as I searched for the key of the safe. Keys rattled in my hands as I brought them nearer to the keyhole. And just when I aspired to put the journal inside, I decided to have one last look within the book that had become the draft of my existence. I skimmed through it, turning the pages like it was a flipbook. And out of nowhere, a single sheet caught my attention. Blood drained from my face as I gawked down onto it with incredulity. A page with a diary entry dated the day after tomorrow.

Chapter Five

Time After Time Again

THERE WAS A TIME IN my life when I wouldn't even have considered it: for a decision so potent to have opted in my reasoning; as it was, this was the first time ever the resolution of renunciation could not escape my logic.

I was forty-three now, and for the last twelve years, I had lived under this illusion that Saturn and I will be together forever and always. But to be thrown back like this, after years, after a decade – to get used to something and then suddenly everything rotated – ultimately broke me. Thus, when the moment had come, and I saw that time in itself had seduced me, I couldn't help averting the judgment. My life had remained, on the other side of the curtain, an act of perpetual misfortune, beating me down to the bone. It was a point where I felt so much chary, that the living in constant fear of meritless deeds (one of the cruellest things I could imagine happening to a person) has ultimately shattered me into pieces.

At its core, I was the one to be held accountable. I couldn't impute anyone else but myself. And I'm sure if Miss Precious had still been around, here with me, she would have tried to convince me otherwise. But the details of my own faults were apparent, I couldn't evade it. There was a time in my life when I had lived irresponsibly, wandering about in time heedless of what the consequences would bear. Living days as if they were absolute. Now, I had to settle. To confess in my unbounded verity, Saturn was not the one leaving my reality; it was I who passed my own fluke. For I lived those days that caused the cease of the surviving relation; the result, my conscious mind travelled to an alternate timeline where once Saturn and I had not yet met again. Tomorrow shall heed in a similar effect.

Gawking onto the page in the journal, I reached for my phone in my pocket. There was only one person I could talk to right now. One person besides Saturn who would be able to help me momentarily. Joy. I dialled his number as rapidly as could in hopes that he'd have something remedial to say. And after I told him everything, his first response was to have a meet-and-greet. I suggested the bar where we always met up, any place other than home.

Water dripped from my hair down onto the ground as I entered the bar a couple of minutes after our brief phone call. It was raining outside, and my taxicab didn't stop near the entrance. It smelled of alcohol and tobacco, and my eyes searched for Joy through the smoke. He waited for me by the bar as he would always do when we met each other here. He glanced towards the entrance as he greeted the bartender and walked towards me.

He greeted warmly, to which I had no response. "Shit, I'm sorry," he continued sympathetically, relatively straight to the point.

We walked directly to an open table, got ourselves two beers (which we drank throughout our conversation), took off our coats, and I went over everything again.

"So, have you thought about what you're going to do now?" Joy asked concerningly.

It was a good question, indeed, and it had two completely different answers. Firstly, preparation. For how does one prepare oneself for something like this to happen: the loss of another to occur? If I had to say it myself, I deem it better, not knowing when something like this will happen. Though the surprise element can ultimately lead to finding ampler closure at ends – I imagined as I bore in mind all the previous times I didn't know when or if Saturn would disappear, and how I then struggled to find peace. Secondly, what will I do after it had happened? Thus, I responded plainly and simply, "I do not know."

"Well, as long as you know that I'm always here for you, Arné. Remember that." He started to sound like Miss Precious, to be honest. And although it had me emotional, I didn't show much of it. But I could regard his keen observation right through me.

There was a moment of silence between us in which we got ourselves a second round of beers. Joy got up and went to the restroom. The gas bubbles, floating from the bottom to the top of the glass, mesmerised my eyes, though like a trance; it sent me into a reverie:

By its cause, two essential things happened to me after Miss Precious had died; as it was, I had seen her death, by the end of my twentieth, as a mere representation of her own future in my present. The ken of her death arrived when I was still exploring and experimenting with my ability to travel in time. I had done so, for the sake of caution, actuating back and forth, always staying within that year I had turned twenty, not going a day earlier nor later; this excluding the two-to-be mentioned exceptional cases. Her death was then, the tore of affiliation, the trigger point towards a crusade for fulfilment.

Her memorial was a day, I had hence never forgotten; not one single detail of it – though I never wished to recall it and though as if it was the outset of any subsequence. Externally, it was a beautiful day too, and yet, within all that beauty arose much deformation and confusion. As it was, nobody showed up for the memorial at the local church, and I didn't know who else to invite except for myself; though one other strange figure hiding at the back of the church did show up towards the end of the ceremony. This external factor was then the reason that internally, a black cloud hung over my head. For it made me think if Miss Precious wasn't this person I had once made her out to be. Her life had become cryptic as mine: an obscure history. Did something happen in her past? Was it sinister and corrupt? Was the excellent treatment of myself a treaty for her own conscience? I couldn't help myself but think this way. I reasoned that the person I knew was righteous, and I would not let this scepticism get the better of her fair image in my views.

By the last words from the reverend's mouth, I stood up and walked towards the door to go and smoke a cigarette (I had started recently).

"Arné?" the strange figure halted me near the door.

"Yes," I said, "that's me. Are you family?" I didn't know what else to say.

The man grinned. "Oh, no!" he said. "An acquaintance, you might say," he said in a ruminative fashion.

I remained silent, speechless, for a moment where I nodded my head before I continued: "Well, have a good day." I walked away.

"Wait," the man halted me once more. I could see he had trouble finding a way to speak his intentions. "I think Precious would have liked for you to have this." He handed me a folded piece of paper and walked away. That was the last time I ever saw him.

As I lit my cigarette outside, I unfolded the piece of paper the man had given me and found myself gawking at an address with a brief script reading '*your biological mother*'. Who was the man? A private investigator Miss Precious knew? Has she arranged for the locating of my biological mother? I don't think she ever stopped seeking the mysteries of my past; this must have been one of those things. I didn't know the answers to my conspiracies, and I never got to elucidate them (like so many other unanswered questions in my life); but so it was that, in my mind, the loss of my mom had brought me the location of my mother. So, by the end of the tragedy, it had left me many woeful affairs, included:

Firstly, the unfulfilling belongings of Miss Precious, which reminded me only of her once presence – she had no other close relatives nor any children of her own, so I was the one to inherit these things – including her suburban home and her capital (which for whatever reason I knew not was a lot more than I had anticipated);

Secondly, the ashes of Miss Precious – which for the most part stood vast in her house until I knew what to do with it; and lastly, was the location of my biological mother.

And though it was all well and satisfactory, the house was too quiet, and life was just as lonesome.

Therefore (back to the original thought), the first essential thing which happened to me after Miss Precious had died, was going back to see what had happened to me that night in the orphanage house. Though the idea was old, it sparked to actuality one lonely evening as I lay on that same old bed I've had since that day I first arrived in Miss Precious's bureau. My eyes were closed. The act called to the day before I met Miss Precious for the first time. My heart started to pound out of the world as I began to feel light-headed. And all of a sudden, the bed escaped my back, though as if I plunged right through it. The drop spiralled into the immediate feeling of halt coming over my body; it heralded the release of a recent tactility from my grasp, though as if I was running with someone hand-in-hand.

A free-spirited adolescent smiling back at me emerged from under a big green tree from the blinding light of a busy sun setting. The figure appeared to be at least fifteen years of age (just like myself). Blue eyes and hair, made out of honey curls, glistened at the sight of dawn. The change to a natural aroma made my nose itchy, and the laughter of the adolescent glancing back at me made me smile. I fell in love, that very instance.

"Come on, Arné!" the adolescent said in front of me, coming to a prolonged standstill.

I was confused; I didn't even know the name of the person talking to me. "Where are we going?" I grinned.

"What do you mean, where are we going?" said the adolescent. "We are going to the green hills, my love, there whence the mountain greets the sky and cries the lake beneath dawn's lonely eye. That place where we can be for our behove." It was said in a rather witty manner but still with good intention.

"Arné, Saturn," a woman suddenly called with a wobbly voice dragging me back to a sense of reality.

I turned around and saw a woman with tanned skin wearing a headscarf, standing on the patio in front of a manor house. She looked taut. "Would you two mind coming in, please?" she said like it wasn't a question. "Principal Malin asked for you."

Two things went through my mind in that instance. The first thing was the name that was called with mine; for I had heard Saturn's name for the first time. The woman who looked taut was the second thing; for now, I had wondered what waited for us on the other side of the back door. I felt a sudden gentle shoulder against mine.

"Well, come on! Miss Hope's looking for us," said Saturn.

We entered the house, and although the room we had entered was significantly big, the circumstances made it feel too small for all the people there. Miss Hope was standing alone on the right side of three men. I recognised one tall and obese man as Principal Malin – and two other strange figures dressed in black, standing behind him.

"Which one is it?" one of the men asked Principal Malin.

"Well, the one with blond hair of course," Principal Malin said straight forward.

I was confused, to say the least, and the fear in Miss Hope's eyes made my heart pound out of this world.

"Go to your room, Arné," said Principal Malin.

Standing on my left side, Saturn was shaking.

"Please don't. Don't go. Don't leave me alone," Saturn whispered into my ear.

I honestly didn't know what to do. So, I hesitated. Should I go and the worst might happen to Saturn, or should I stay and try to prevent it from happening.

"Would you please just go to your room?" Principal Malin shouted angrily. It gave Saturn, Miss Hope, and myself a startle, but still, I stayed unmoved. "Miss Hope, would you please escort Arné to his room," he continued in a calmer voice.

But Miss Hope also delayed in his command. I could see that she was as confused as I was and as scared as Saturn. "What is the meaning of this?" she said.

Troubled by what Miss Hope had just said, Principal Malin made a sign towards the two strange men. "Why do I always have to beg you bitch to do anything!" he said.

Miss Hope was disturbed by what he had said. The two men each individually walked to both Saturn and me. I moved towards Saturn, trying to block the two men from taking Saturn, but they quickly came to separate us. They were strong, and although I wanted to fight it, it was worthless.

"Arné!" cried Saturn.

I tried to fight some more, but the strange man holding me pressed a damp cloth against my mouth, and I was forced to inhale the drug he had put on it. Time lengthened as everything I saw appeared to move in one blurring panorama. The last thing I could remember before waking up the following morning to the sound of sirens screaming in my ears was one previous cry from Saturn calling my name.

Saturn's body was found the next morning by the police in the lake surrounded by the mountain and the hills near the orphanage house. *'A robbery has gone wrong'* was the headlines I overheard, stated by the news broadcasting services reporting on the tragedy. I didn't know how they had come to find the body of that beautiful soul, with whom I fell in love with the first time, my conscious mind acknowledged our reception. Though, I was glad to see Principal Malin caught for it; but there was never any two strange men along with it mentioned. It appeared though they had vanished into the darkness with the artefact they had taken from Saturn.

I quickly went back to my room, where I lay before I had travelled in time; where I was twenty-one again. The events which had occurred in that short period had come to crush my spirit. So, on a mission to find closure and sentiment, it was that looking for and finding my biological mother was the second most crucial thing that had happened to me after Miss Precious had died.

I still heard the echo of her voice in my head. "You might not think this, Arné, but you're an extraordinary person. I had come to care for you a lot, like a son. I do consider you to be my own," she told me one day after I had told her my secret.

And although Miss Precious was, and always will be, the closest thing I will ever have of something I could call Mom, finding my biological mother was something I felt not needed to be done, but rather something I wanted to do, now more than ever. And so it was that the small piece of paper with the erudition of my mother I inherited, suddenly became my only hope for clarity and closure. I didn't need time travelling to find her; she lived in a city not far from where I lived.

And within a day, I found myself an evening where I stood in front of her suburban house overlooking the agnostic possibility of where I once should have been present. I knocked on the front door of the house, but nobody came. I admitted that nobody was at home. But I wasn't going to give up that easily. There was a bus stop located on the other side of the road, and I decided to wait there for a while just to see if anybody might show up. After an hour, I had convinced myself that nobody will come, and I should instead leave it till the day after. But just before I wanted to go, a car had parked right in front of the house. I was eager to see who it was and if by chance, it was my mother, what she looked like. A woman was driving, and a young man was sitting in the passenger seat next to her. They climbed out. Everything about her was beautiful; from her dark hair, to how she dressed. And although she and the young man had appeared to be in an argument, she still seemed to be elegant. I was jealous of the young man who was with her, whoever he might have been. They went into the house, and I watched them through the kitchen window.

Finally, I convinced myself to go in. But just as I crossed the road, the woman walked out of the front door with two garbage bags, one in each hand. I was approaching the sidewalk right in front of the house when I convinced myself otherwise. A sudden change of heart. Timid. I was too weak to introduce myself. Hence, I pretended that I was on my way to some other destination. To be frank, I was alarmed, to say the least, and I didn't know any more if I indeed required to find out the truth. Though as if not knowing, it might have led me to someplace more fortunate. But it didn't matter what I thought, for she acknowledged me with a nod, though as if she knew I saw them arguing.

"Kids," she grinned.

At that moment, I broke one more time. For the closeness of the motherly figure resembled that of my own. It was also that closeness which was why I couldn't go to look for Saturn at the conservatory every time Saturn had disappeared. For the acknowledgement of her figure made it familiar (only later), she was the conservatory's secretary – and I couldn't face her every time I had met Saturn.

Nonetheless, there I stood in front of her, my biological mother, and I thought, *why me? Why was I the one to be tossed away?* It didn't make sense, though I didn't expect anything less, for most things in my life, didn't make any sense.

Yet, I replied with all that anguish in mind, out of the habit of politeness. "I wouldn't know." I tried to fake a smile.

She pouched her lips as I spoke. "I haven't seen you around here," she said. "Do you live nearby?" She was sociable. I didn't know many people who would just walk up to a stranger and begin a conversation like this, but it might have been the type of neighbourhood too.

"Just visiting," I said.

"Family or friends?" she asked me.

I didn't know how to answer that question. "I guess you could say both," I said vaguely.

She tightened her lips again after my reply.

"Good," she said. "Well, you enjoy yourself and take care, and be careful like this all alone out here by yourself," her motherly tone had me almost in tears, but I tried not to show emotion.

Why would you care now? I thought. "I will do that, Ma'am," I said and went back the way I had come from, as she also went back into the house.

I wanted to go back home, but I didn't feel like walking, so I waited for the bus to come, and I lit myself a cigarette to let the time go by faster. The man and woman's argument had continued, and a few minutes later, with no bus in sight, the young man walked out of the front door and walked straight towards me.

"Hi, bro," he greeted me like a teenager. "Can I borrow your lighter?" he asked politely. He must have seen me smoking myself.

Without hesitation, I took it out and lent it to him. His green eyes had him look more handsome up closer than he appeared from afar, and his dark hair resembled mine.

"Mothers," he said. "Am I right?" He laughed and handed me my lighter back.

"I wouldn't know," I said as I glanced at him, taking a pull of my cigarette. My response made him feel uncomfortable. It made me feel uncomfortable too.

"My mom doesn't know that I smoke," he said, seemingly to try and change the topic of the conversation we apparently had. He looked ashamed, but I knew it wasn't his fault.

So, I nodded. "Mine too," I replied, and it was the truth, trying to make him feel more at ease, and then I smiled. Before I left, my bus approached, and I had one last question I needed to know the answer to. "So, where's your father?"

"Do not have one," he replied. "Mother fucker left."

And as my bus pulled over, I greeted him. "Know the feeling," I said as I climbed in.

The city lights calmed me in a way as I stared at them on my route home. I knew that it was time. I could have asked every question I had ever wanted to ask my mother. But I had decided not to for one good reason; I had realised that it doesn't matter. Not anymore, anyway. Not now. I'll never be able to change the past and what had happened.

So, those were the two essential things that had happened to me after Miss Precious had died. They left me both changed and scared at the same time. Changed, for I had witnessed the inevitable. Scared, for I had not known what my future held. Though I knew I was alone. So, they had me by the throat. And I turned to that one thing, so many before me had turned to, to pass my life. I started to drink; ignorant of what consequences it will bear, I went rogue: travelling back and forth in time like life had no more meaning for me.

Almost a century passed by me like a beam of light without any proper function, nor destination (something that transpires with so many others, I bet you know). Not even paying attention to the days I had lived, and the days I had not lived. Until I was a hundred and twenty-year-old, living in a nursing home with a minimum account of what the outside world resembled. And I did try to travel past that age, but I couldn't. Though as if there were, in fact, some unspoken logic behind my gift. A scientific natural law, or something, preventing me from growing older than that. I have to add that a century sounds like much. But when I think back to it now, it feels like it had fallen within a blink of an eye.

Nevertheless, it was the evening before I turned one year older, and I knew I was dying. Not only because I had not seen the proceeding times, but I could also strangely feel it in my body. The doctors and nurses at the nursing home knew it too.

"I'm afraid he won't make it through the night," bedridden, I overheard a nurse talking outside my room. She was speaking to what sounded like an intern or something.

I will have to lie if I say that I haven't thought about death and what it would be like.

The other whispered something I couldn't make out.

"He's got Alzheimer's, my dearie," she said again.

And, oh boy, did I want to raise my voice. If only the people here had known the truth. But I was too weak to do or say anything. Fortunately, I thought it; for I didn't want Alzheimer's and be a mad man all at the same time. They left me. I did die that evening. Physically, though, not consciously. But I remember nothing about it at all, for so it was that it had happened in my sleep.

After falling asleep, I could remember the next thing, bedridden in that lonesome bed, walking in the rain. I was eager to see where I'll end up after dying; usually, I would think of the time I would like to live. It took me a moment to recognise the place. Rain ran down the street like a river in the middle of the neighbourhood I was in, and the streetlights familiarised the suburban houses.

New City's outer regions, I told myself.

From the sidewalk, my gaze was fixed to the other side of the road—a stare of brink astonishment. For what I saw was Miss Precious through a window, which reflected my age. I must have been twenty-one again. Not even a minute after that, I found myself soaking wet, knocking on the front door of that old suburban house I had come to know as home. The door swung open as I was greeted with two arms gently pressing me against a warm figure.

Miss Precious's eyes bestowed no ignorance. She must have seen the transformation I had borne.

"My goodness, Arné," she said very much concerningly.

"I needed to see you," I started to cry.

Her arms greeted me again as she let me in. A few minutes had passed when the warm glow of flames dried my face, and a towel thrown around my shoulders kept me warm. I stared into the fire as the clinking of silverware to my ears relaxed me. Miss Precious came out of the kitchen with two cups of tea. And there we sat for a while longer in silence.

"How long has it been," she said, not even bothering to ask the question of what had transpired, although I knew that was coming soon.

"Almost ninety years," I replied. My answer as short as my thoughts were.

"My goodness, Arné," she said again taking my hand. "And what were you doing all that time?" she asked. Her eyes showing deep affection of warmth and serenity.

"I—I…" I tried to speak, but nothing had come out for a while as I stared back into the fire. "Drinking, mostly," I said.

"I see," she said. "And if I may ask, why?"

"For I had seen too much I could bear," I said gravely.

She left it there, and although we did have the conversation about both the orphanage house and my mother a few days later, she asked me another question I wasn't ready to give an answer to. I answered as vaguely as I could. For she asked me how I had come to survive all those years, and my answer was as short and nebulous as possible: "You left me some."

"I see," she said for I could see from how I had spoken those words; she knew I was talking about her own death. "And how did you find yourself back here?"

"For I had seen my own," I said morosely. "I had seen my own fortune. And it had changed me, I feel like a coward," I cried.

In that instance, she had taken me up in her arms, holding me like she had never before. "You will not repeat such a thing ever again, Arné, do you hear me," she said. "You are anything but, nothing even close to something like that."

We didn't talk much after that, and I went straight to bed after she had me calm enough. But before I fell asleep, one last thought had entered my mind. It was my journal. The same book Miss Precious had given me all those years back. I was drawn to its theory. Though as if it was mystical, it was a time moment. I found it in my nightstand drawer and opened it, for I felt the need to write in it. Even if it were only one word. But as I did open it, I had found myself, in another time, to have already written therein.

For in an impeccable life, we would have found each other, and for that perfect day, I shall always strive.

The few months following the day I returned, had come to be some of the best days of my entire life. I had spent all of them with Miss Precious. And though they were all good, the best was a time she told me: "You do that, Arné, you create your own happiness." It arrived just after I had told her everything about my past, and I told her of a plan. A scenario in which I shall set off and save

Saturn, and then search for Saturn afterwards. By the end of my twentieth anniversary and the end of Miss Precious's life, I bought the orphanage house in which I grew up, sprinkled Miss Precious's ashes under that tree where I first met Saturn and went back to the year in which I turned nine.

And so, there I stood in front of the manor house, meeting Miss Hope. For seven years, I stayed there, in the orphanage house and all its gloom; until it burned down at its end, just before I had managed to save Saturn. Directly after that, I turned to the year just after Miss Precious had passed, and I commenced my search for Saturn.

Since it is important, I have to add that I did see Miss Precious again. In fact, I had come to look for Saturn in these years. Though not after my twenty-first birthday – but I suppose I had forgotten about a day I didn't live in my twentieth year. By then, I was used to waking up in different timelines because of what I had done. And so, on the day of its occurrence, I remembered running down the stairs, smelling breakfast. My eyes quickly met Miss Precious's, and by my astonishment, I knew that she knew.

"Arné?" she said.

I remained silent.

"Is everything okay?" she said again.

I remained silent.

"This is not your timeline, is it?"

I shook my head. "I can't believe that it's actually you." I hugged her. "I miss you."

She cancelled her errands for the day, and we spent it together. And the last question she asked of me was: "Have you found Saturn yet?"

"No..." I said with disappointment.

"Well, you just keep on looking," she inspired me.

I was drawn back to reality as Joy patted me on my shoulder and came to sit next to me again. "I think that it's time to leave it," I uttered without even thinking what I was saying.

"Leave what?" Joy asked curiously.

"Everything," I said. "I thought that I'll take Saturn and the two children tomorrow evening to the garden and wait it out. And after that, I think that it will be better for me to leave."

He looked at me sympathetically. "Are you sure that's what you want to do?" he asked.

"I think that's what I must do," though I didn't feel like it, that's what I replied.

"If that's what you want, Arné."

"It is," I said. "But I do have something to ask you, though."

"Anything."

"Will you look after Saturn for me while I'm gone," I lamented.

"Of course, Arné," he said. "Just tell me the same thing back in your new timeline."

I smiled. It was smart of Joy to say that. And it made me think why he never disappeared like Saturn did; for I had met him before I went rogue.

Chapter Six

Love Renewed

THESE DAYS I REFLECTED, AND I often mused over fortune. And I considered: if a person had come to know their own fortune, would they still choose to live it twice? If not, how does one choose between timelines? How would you measure the most salutary from the most acute, and how does one know which one shall present you with the most joy? Although we all do get to choose between them, as we all have our alternatives and make our decisions between them every day of our lives, we do not get to see their different outcomes. My own eyes have always been exceedingly fixed on the other results, rather than finding pleasure within the journey. This, to such a point where I had ultimately forgotten to actually live. I see now that although the ending does hold a considerable amount of significance, it is the journey in which we experience joy. That was the closing remarks I acknowledged as the end of the 12-year journey approached.

I headed straight back home after Joy and I talked; there where I made love to Saturn one last time, and the following beautiful morning while I was preparing breakfast Saturn came into the kitchen and greeted me with a kiss.

"That smells nice," Saturn said and went on pouring us both a cup of filter coffee.

I grinned. "Thank you," I said. "Did you sleep well?"

"Lovely," Saturn smiled and gave me another kiss.

"That's good." I smiled back.

"So, any big plans for the day?"

I heard Saturn Jr. and Chris waking up and coming downstairs. "I actually wanted to talk to you about that."

"Yes, I'm listening?" Saturn sat at the kitchen counter.

"I was wondering if we could maybe do something together, all of us?"

"What's the occasion?" Saturn interrupted.

"Nothing special. Would just like to spend a day away from the drag."

"What did you have in mind?"

"I don't know. I was thinking about the beach?"

"Oh, wow. That's a three-hour drive. And only for one day?"

From the stairs, Saturn Jr and Chris walked into the kitchen, joining the conversation.

"Beach?" greeted Chris.

Saturn made a face at me. "I don't know. What do you think, Sats? Do you think your dad has gone mad to only go to the beach for the day?"

Saturn Jr smiled. "Isn't the worst idea he's ever had."

"Well, that settles it," said Saturn. "I guess we're going to the beach for the day."

And it was a beautiful day, hence. By the night-drive back home, everybody was fast asleep in the car – Saturn in the passenger seat next to mine, and Saturn Jr and Chirs aback behind us. The rearview mirror showcased the image of the privileged future I will soon be left out of. And I wondered who our children will grow up to be and what they will be like; their graduations, weddings, and children... These thoughts elapsed the three-hour ride back to New City, and as I pulled the car over, Saturn woke up.

"Are we home already?" Saturn said sleepily.

"Not yet," I said, "I thought about one last stop."

"But, honey, it's late," yawned Saturn. It was almost midnight.

"I know, I know," I said as I took Saturn's hand. "Please, just for a while."

"Okay, but only for a few minutes," said Saturn. "Where are we, by the way?"

"The botanical garden," I said as I got out of the car. Saturn followed, we woke Saturn Jr and Chris as we took them from the car and went in.

The garden looked like any other of its sort. However, the florae were ever greener and excelled their distinct colours, as it had rained a moment before we had arrived. The sound of water running over beautifully stacked rocks created calming waterfalls and the art amidst the garden gave it a well-meditative mood. I was intrigued by the landscape where I stood. The wind brushed through the leaves of two beautiful trees in front of me – one slightly bigger than the other – and a red wall stood fast behind them with nothing growing in their surroundings. It made me reflect. I had come to think of it as nature versus civilisation; were the two able to stand in peace and harmony with each other, or was it barely an illusion portrayed by its beautiful appearance? I drew a comparison from my own life – life as the most natural thing I could come to think of, was it still a beautiful thing, as unnatural as it had happened? Nevertheless, my thoughts quickly changed as I heard a voice approaching me from afar.

"Papa!" she shouted.

It was as soft and gentle as the breeze which had carried it. And with this new thought of love, I wondered if life would ever be so kind as to make me meet love as high as that ever again. I turned my head around, and as I laid my eyes upon Chris, I smiled. Her two feet met the grass beneath them gracefully, one after the other. I turned myself around and placed my arms out in front of me. As she reached me, I swung her around myself, throwing her up into the air – never letting her go entirely from my grasp – and caught her again. I was holding a miracle in my arms, along with her elegant smile. Chris was four at the time.

She laughed. "I brought you a flower, Papa," she said as her light brown eyes were fixed upon the lavender.

"I see, my darling," I said. "It's beautiful." And it was lovely, just like her smile.

She knew how much I adored lavender, for she had always gone to get me some from whatever garden we were at. But like any other child her age though, she was quickly distracted. Her attention shifted to her brother. Saturn Jr. was eleven years old. The wind brushed through his long cut hair, and the night made it appear darker than it actually was. He was quiet for a boy his age, and even more this evening. However, they were both intrigued by the florae and faunas the garden had offered. It kept them busy for a while, as I watched how they played together. It made me happy. Their innocence brought enormous amounts of joy into my life, yet they had to pay within that innocence. Though only in my mind. For they shall continue like nothing has changed, and I, with my consciousness, shall leave. For a moment, I had forgotten the real reason for our visit. The realisation of my ignorance drew my eyes towards my wrists. I gasped as I read the time to myself: it was practically midnight.

"Papa, look," Chris shouted out of nowhere, and then a stick broke behind me.

I turned around. And amazed, I saw Saturn standing in front of me, at least ten years younger. And with that appearance came the ignorance; for Saturn's eyes showed no recognition. It had me baffled. For, the effect had already taken influence, yet the children were still here – though as if everything had happened in slow motion. Also, to note that Saturn didn't vanish.

"I see," I quickly told Chris.

And I kept calm. I didn't want the children confused, or as scared as I was, so I tried to fake my emotions for as long as possible. Chris started to run towards me. I thought her startled, though as if she didn't know what was going on.

"Look what Saturn has, Chirs," I showed her towards her older brother, trying to distract her.

But she didn't listen (like most children her age), she did the exact opposite. She went to Saturn instead. I quickly followed. Chris tried to give Saturn the lavender, and I heard Saturn saying, "it's my favourite." Then she let me share the flower with Saturn instead.

"I have to go," Saturn suddenly said.

I didn't know what to say. For a moment, I gazed upon our children, and with the preconceived knowledge of their disappearance that will soon conspire, and that I will be alone shortly; I uttered, "No. Don't. Please. I mean, stay. I don't want to be alone."

Saturn looked confused. And as Chris went away to play with her brother, I proceeded to sit on a bench a few feet away from where we were standing. Saturn followed. We sat, and I glanced towards my wrist. *Virtually midnight*, I told myself. And with a glance up, I beheld Chirs and Saturn's disappearance.

"Where are they?" Saturn said with confusion and wide eyes.

I knew that very instance; Saturn had too noticed my own transformation: I was twenty-nine; at least fifteen years younger.

"Gone," I said sadly.

Chapter Seven

A Sense of Belonging

THERE WAS A TIME IN my life when I had feared to be alone, nowadays it was all I ever wanted. I had never really, fully comprehended the perils of placing your happiness and joy in the hands of another. And although I shall never come to succumb of it, for Saturn was and always will be my salvation, I had to leave. I had to go and find my own sense again; for too long, I had forgotten it.

That was why, when the time came, I left that night in the Botanical Garden, without Saturn by my side. Then, I headed straight to that place I had once – long ago – promised myself I'll never return to, the orphanage house in Old Town. It wasn't an orphanage house anymore because I had bought it (for what seemed in my mind a very long time ago, when, in reality, it had only been around 8 years). I did so when I was still twenty-one, intending to transform it into something more beautiful. Bountiful. Something to attempt to reshape the past. Though it always reminded me of Saturn. And yet now, when I think back on it, Saturn was my job, my leisure, and my life. Or that was what I considered Saturn to be. But for too long had I forgotten about ascertaining myself. In a sense, also, I thought I failed my own life; to lead the rest of a peaceful one, I had to make the most of what I had left (which was only two conscious years). It goes without saying that my life had been a rather mess, a series of displacements. With this final effort, I would grant myself the last resting place before I too leave this world behind.

It was the day just after I lost all of them, Saturn, Saturn Jr. and Chris, and there I stood, having climbed out of my car, in front of the gate of that old orphanage house. A lean man in his thirties approached me from a distance. He was still muscular, though you could see that he indulged in many strenuous hand activities.

The keys rattled in his hands, having taken them off his belt. "Good day, Arné," he said and unlocked the gate. "I didn't think that we'll see you back here so soon." He laughed.

I liked his humour a lot; it was one of the first things I acknowledged before hiring him as the foreman of the farm. His freshest joke was amusing for two reasons: I haven't been here ever since I bought the place, and I left him in charge of everything; and the irony that for him only 8 years have passed, whereas – for myself – a couple more.

"Hello, Earnest, " I greeted back. "Nor did I," I played along as I aided him in pulling the gates open before I greeted him with the hand. "So, how have you been?"

"No worries," he said. "Just busy as always."

"That's good to hear," I said. "And your wife?"

"Pregnant," he replied quickly.

It made me think about what I just lost. "Well! Congratulations." I patted him on his shoulder.

"Yeah, five months now."

"And the pregnancy is going well?"

"Yeah, no drag. All good."

"That is good to hear," I said and started to walk to my car. "Come on, let's go. I'll give you a lift. You can catch me up on everything."

Earnest closed the gate behind the car and got in. The gravel road amid the purple blossoming lavenders, which lead to the mansion, mesmerized my eyes as Earnest spoke to me about the farm, telling me everything I needed to know. And upon reaching their own residence, Verity (Earnest's wife) met us out front.

Their intimate farmhouse was about a kilometre away from the manor that was still in sight through thick leaves of trees, thicket and shrubs in the front garden.

"Ary," Verity greeted me after I pulled over. "What a pleasant surprise. So lovely to see you." The way she said my name made me smirk. She was as quirky in the pregnancy as she was before it. And it made me smile some more due to her glow within the fertility, dressed in a colourful maternity skirt and some sandals.

"Always a pleasure, Verity," I grinned as I climbed out of the car.

The usual pleasantries followed as Earnest unloaded my bags from the trunk.

"I assume you'll be staying here with us?"

"Just for a week or two. Until I have at least my room and kitchen functioning."

"Don't forget a bathroom," she joked. "But you could stay for as long as you like. What do you say, Eary."

"Any time," Earnest said as he patted me on the back. "Just glad to see that we will see something done to the house," he continued flippantly as he dragged my bags into the house.

I gave Earnest strict instructions not to restore the manor (any building needed to maintain the farm, except for the estate). As it was, the house was still empty, laying in ruin after the fire. Though there wasn't anything wrong with the construction, nor the foundation (as I had a constructor examine it), yet it sprawled in eagerness, awaiting restoration.

The evening was festive both around the dinner table where we enjoyed a meal Verity had prepared for us, and in the living room where we skipped from subject to subject, indulging in gaining conversation. Two weeks afterwards, after long hours and hard labour, some places in the house were finally inhabitable; suitable to live in, though there were still loads to be done. Hence, I stayed there for one year, preoccupied with renovating the house and working on the farm. So, I meditated – renewing myself. I was a farmer who amused himself with quiet evenings and books and enjoyed the occasional visits to and from Earnest, Verity, and their newborn baby girl, Alina. But – not expecting anything less – just as I got used to this new life, it came to throw me back against the wall one more time.

Chapter Eight

———

Left to be Used

A *MURDER WILL BE COMMITTED tomorrow evening in the orphanage house. The body of the child will be found near the orphanage house by the lake surrounded by the mountain and hills.*

These were some of the information Arné's account provided in which he had beheld this dreadful event once before. The journal he had once mysteriously found underneath his pillowcase on his bed was more than a simplistic diary; he always carried it around with him, wherever he went. He had often thought about the coming evening. But he had never thought about it as much as he did lately. Especially tonight.

The orphanage house (also a school situated near a coastal town called Old Town) held its annual recital that evening. Arné was pinned into one of the corners of that school hall's foyer like a startled pup awaiting release. He breathed heavily. His right hand was clammy from clenching the journal against his chest. People pushed and jolted forward; they rubbed against each other – and worse, they rubbed against him – making their way towards the school hall in an excelling zest to get a good seat for tonight's concert. It all made him clasp onto his journal, tighter with every passing second. He couldn't lose it; not tonight. For therein was a letter of precious value that he had to deliver to its legitimate receiver.

You would think that this kind of people would behave according to how they dress, he felt within that moment. It was somewhat ironic that seeing men in bowties and women in dresses acting like this. But what irritated him even more, was the things they said.

"Well, I do pity these children. The poor things."

"I know. I wish I could do more."

Suddenly, within all that chaos, Arné got a sudden relief of tension. Adrenaline shot through his veins as they released fluttering butterflies in his stomach. He saw his saviour: Saturn had just walked through the doors of the foyer. It almost made him shout out loud in that instance. But he didn't. It merely made him revere for the first couple of seconds, almost like he had opened his eyes, again, for the very first time. "Saturn!" Arné then shouted, trying to catch Saturn's attention. But nothing was accomplished; the crowd's uttering was too loud, and his cry was too soft.

Saturn tried to stand still within the moving crowd, though, trying to perceive Arné's appearance – knowing that he would have come early tonight and waited. The assembly always kept on pushing forwards, so Saturn was ultimately forced to move along with it.

"Saturn!" Arné cried again. He sprang and tried to shovel himself through the masses. But the room was too big, the crowd too thick, and he too slow. He clenched his fist in dismay as he looked on: Saturn disappeared through the doors of the hall.

Arné's eyes widened when it was finally his turn to go in. There were people everywhere, still pushing and rubbing and jolting against each other – against him. He didn't like it. Not in the slightest. It made him feel small and weak; he wasn't able to control any of it. But that quickly changed when he spotted Saturn, sitting in one of the front row seats reserved for all the children who were about to perform. And although he knew that he won't sit there next to Saturn, it gave him a sense of calm when he saw Saturn so benign. He breathed out; his muscles relaxed. He quickly found himself another seat not far from Saturn. And there he sat with his two arms gently hugging his journal against his chest.

An interval of silence spread throughout the hall. The lights were dimmed. And not long after that, everybody watched a middle-aged man, followed by a spotlight, walking up onto the stage.

"Welcome, ladies and gentlemen, to this year's annual orphanage recital!" he boasted on centre stage. "My name is Principal Malin, and I am the headmaster of this spectacular school."

The crowd applauded. As it appeared, Principal Malin had an excellent reputation with these people (*the people from the town,* as the children would call them); his attitude, tonight, not saying anything less than that. But this was not the case for the children. They knew the truth. They knew the true colours of the man who stood in front of them, pretending to be something that he was not. Arné was no exception to this. He felt a great deal of contempt as he looked towards Principal Malin with a tight-lipped smile. He was yet again forced to indulge in one of his speeches. Not that he listened or paid any attention in the slightest. For his attention was converged onto Saturn, to such an extent that the applause of the final worlds of Principal Malin's opening had left him incredulous.

"Miss Hope, everybody!" Principal Malin announced.

A woman dressed in a green dress and a matching headscarf stood up from among the audience. Every child in the hall sat up straight upon hearing Miss Hope's name. She glided onto the platform like a feather in a gentle breeze, broadening every smile that noticed her that evening. She was the image of pure aspiration like her name suggested.

She presented herself, continuing with the first couple of performers' introductions, each at their appropriate time. And about five performances into the program, Saturn was finally summoned. The applause of Saturn's name inclined fame. Bright-eyed and bushy tailed, Arné turned his head sideways to indulge in the elevated moment. But out of nowhere, within the movement of turning his head to his right, he got a fright. A sense of discomfort took over him. For what he saw was a written image being manifested in front of his own very two eyes. They looked just like his journal had portrayed them; the two strange men. He flung his head to the front, thinking of shouting out the truth. But how could he? They had not done anything wrong. Not yet anyway. And if he would have shouted something, everybody would have looked at him like a needy child who's going deranged. Arné struggled to let it go. And though he had not wholly come to let it go since, watching Saturn walking up onto the stage made him feel that same feeling he had felt earlier that evening again. It made him feel like everything will be okay.

Curtains opened, and they presented an old, but beautiful, upright piano in the centre of the stage. Saturn went to sit in front of it, breathing in and out softly and slowly. Arné closed his eyes. Sound. It was like the echo of water within all its perfect arrangements: rain falling and waves crashing, rivers flowing and waterfalls splashing. And as the strings released music, so were every tension in both Arné's body and mind. He breathed in. And as he breathed out, he was thrown into a reverie:

Arné, being nine at the time, remembered Miss Hope's soft and gentle voice receiving him for the first time. "It's okay, darling," she said.

He remembered only staring at her for the first seconds of their confluence. His eyes, almost tearful, meeting her for the very first time, and just like her name had suggested, he felt a sense of hope. She had, as he revered upon it now, lived up to every single expectation – the most unique and impressionable descriptions imaginable – that his journal presented him with; from the very first second.

"You are safe here," she said and ushered him through the front doors of the orphanage house.

It was somewhat ironic of her to say that, Arné thought. For nothing about it was accurate. It was all a deception. Lies: a story that has been told to her; a trick she had come to believe. But how could she have known that which Arné knew? He, therefore, forgave her in that instance. Not only because she didn't realise it, but also because her words gave him a sense of closure, a sense of calm, and a sense of belonging – almost like the truth.

The entrance hall smelled like an old farmhouse, and loud children stumbled over the carpeted floor. To his left, a skinny man wearing a brown suit approached them from a staircase. He and Miss Hope exchanged pleasantries and then she continued by introducing Arné.

"Hello, Arné," the man greeted him. He went down onto one of his knees and looked Arné in his eyes. "My name is Malin, and I am the principle here of this school and house father of the orphanage." He was manipulatively friendly and kind. His hand caressed Arné's shoulder, almost like he wanted to give him a hug. "I think that we're going to be the greatest of friends," he said.

Arné faked a smile and remained silent although Principal Malin's words had sent shivers down his spine. *If only he had known*, Arné thought. Arné's strange behaviour didn't make anything of Principal Malin. On the contrary, he must have been used to children entering the orphanage for the very first time like this – frightened and abandoned.

Principal Malin continued by smiling, and then he stood up from his knee. "May I have a word, Miss Hope?"

Miss Hope nodded and just before she and Principal Malin left, she looked at Arné and grinned as she let go of his hand. "Go on, Honey. Go on and explore," she said. "I'll be with you again in just a moment."

The house wasn't something extraordinary in Arné's opinion (which was a bit bias if he should've admitted it); he wasn't intrigued by the vintage architecture and delicate marble and wooden decorations inside, but it was big, and he liked that. He followed a partially timbered hallway with paintings hanging against its walls. The floor was mostly wood, and the shared dormitories and rooms he passed smelled of old carpet mats and lumber. The sonance of children moving around and conversing followed him everywhere, in which he did not engage himself. The grownups stared in disgust, though as if their eyes said: 'Yet another one we have to look after. It would've been better if the newling could just drop dead.' He started to look for a way outside. *I was glad to have some time to myself,* he thought. Not because he wanted to be separate, on the contrary, it allowed him to look for someone dear to his heart. Every niche and passage he passed and entered and moved through resembled its own style: the dormitories, which didn't look homey with their double steel beds and cold covers, the dining hall with wooden tables and wooden stools with no backrests, and then the living areas; clean and comfy, though as if they were reserved for the elderly or guests to make it all seem charming.

Arné squinted his eyes as the door behind him closed; the sun was blinding but warm and relaxing on his cheeks. The disgusting smells of the house disappeared; it felt good to breathe in the outdoor air. His eyes took a while to adjust. When they finally did, he got a glimpse of a child lying underneath a big old green tree. And so, it had come that he had found what he was looking for. Beauty redefined itself upon that glance. Without thinking twice, he went over to the child, not having thought it thoroughly through.

"Hi, Saturn," he said timidly. "May I sit with you?"

It took Saturn a few seconds to reply lying still on the grass. "You may do whatever you like. Don't let me stop you," Saturn said rather calmly with closed eyes. "But if you do decide to sit down next to me, maybe then you could tell me why it is that you know my name, but I do not know yours."

Arné grinned. "My name is Arné," he said and sat down on the grass next to Saturn.

"And how do you know me?" Saturn asked before Arné could continue to say anything else.

"Well," Arné hesitated for a second. "I don't know— I don't think that you would believe me. Even if I did tell you."

"Clearly you only know my name then," Saturn said, still lying on the ground. "You only know my name. Because if you did know me, you wouldn't have said that."

"And what if I tell you that I come from the future?" said Arné.

"Then I would say that I believe you," Saturn said and sat up straight.

The sound of hands clapping replaced that of music; it dragged Arné back into reality, and the next thing he saw was Saturn bowing in front of the crowd. The evening, too, soon came to an end after that. The bunch of people sped out of the hall as abruptly as they had entered, and the children remained seated. You would think they would at least stay and congratulate the performers before they did. But there was none of that. They simply just went. Arné walked to the front of the hall where the performers were sitting. Saturn glued to the chair gazed fixedly upon the stage, though as if it rendered a sense of rehabilitation of a showcased and used child.

"You played beautifully," said Arné.

Saturn's gaze turned to him. "You think so," Saturn said and got up. "Or are you just saying that because you don't want to make me feel just awful? I bet you drifted off again into your own world as I played, or even when the others had performed."

Arné blushed and grinned, speechlessly, and the two children shared an agile laugh. He was amazed by Saturn's ability to look right through him like that.

"Don't worry," Saturn said. "I'll play for you again some other time. And maybe then you won't."

Arné smiled. "I'd love that," he said.

They both turned their heads facing aback. The hall was almost cleared from the denseness of the masses. They settled for a while longer before they decided to go out themselves.

"I see that you brought your journal with you again tonight," said Saturn.

Arné looked at it for a while. "Yeah," he said and didn't know what else to say.

Saturn recognised Arné's embarrassment and dropped the topic. "Come, let's get out of here."

The room was cleared when the children started to approach their different dorms. Arné and Saturn, no differently, made small-talk on their way. He had thought about his journal ever since he met Saturn after the concert. His hands had reached for it many times over on their route, overthinking the presentation of the letter. And every time he thought it was the right time, he resisted. Hesitated. Though as if he was afraid. And just before they said goodnight before entering their separate dorms, he tried to give Saturn the letter one last time. But out of nowhere, he stammered, thrown under the covers of his own entanglement of feelings and emotions: loss and fright. *What will Saturn think? How could I, after all this time, just give something like this to somebody, without any personal explanation.* Though as if the moral thing to do would be to sit down and discuss it. But where would he find the words to express his sentiments now? These thoughts and feelings were nothing else but a resistance. The reaction of addressing bad news or converse sensitive discourse emerging ignorant performance – procrastination: the anticipation of the apparent seemingly non-arrival space in time. (He assumed that he's not the only one) *but why do we resist the evident and straightforward; why do we complicate our thoughts and emotions, and toy with them until we grudge?*

"Arné," he suddenly heard Saturn calling his name.

Trapped in his thoughts, he didn't listen again. He looked up.

"I was saying goodnight."

"Oh yeah, sorry. Goodnight."

Saturn looked at Arné concerningly. "Is everything okay? Is there something you would like to talk to me about?"

Arné reached for his journal again. "No," he said pensively. "No, I'm just tired."

BOOK II

———

A Dream Forgotten

POV Saturn exc. 9 & 16

Chapter Nine

Left to Go Away

THE CLOCK TICKED ON; TOMORROW evening is slithering nearer. *Wake up!* Arné startled from his slumber. Pretending to be asleep, he had drifted off with one single thought in mind: he had to give Saturn the letter. But before he was going to do so, he needed to show Saturn the authenticity of the matter. For the letter would make no sense if he didn't. The two walked hand in hand. What worth would the letter then be if he didn't?

It was early the following morning, though it was still dark out; the birds singing were already inaugurating the day alive. Arné's head falling sideways forced him to glance upon his nightstand; it brought him face to face to the letter still resting in his journal – untouched. The bedcovers started to scratch him uncomfortably. He needed to get out of bed. The journal's cold-hard cover stimulated his hand as he took it and unwaveringly drew the bedcovers from his body. He couldn't make a sound and risk waking up the other children in his dorm. When he was finally out of the room, his nightgown followed him like a cape as his bare toes carried him swiftly over the cold wooden floors of the orphanage house. Up the staircases. Down the hallways. Rapidly over the moonlight through the windows casting shadows to fall from the walls between them. And whenever he got to a corner, he would cautiously peek around it to see if anyone was coming. He couldn't get caught; not tonight. The consequences were over explicit: for if they should find him, who knew what might happen – not only to him but to Saturn as well.

Finally, his efforts paid off as he pushed the door of Saturn's dorm ajar. "Sats," he whispered. He turned his head sideways to see if anybody was coming. Then he continued, whispering his rhyme as he would always do, "Sats. Let's set forth to the great green hills, my love. Let's set forth whence the mountain greets the sky and cries the lake beneath dawn's lonely eye. Let's set forth thence to be for our behove."

Suddenly, just after the poem's fulfilment, Arné's worst nightmare of the moment came true. Voices. Horrid vocals echoing down the hallway towards him. He was dumbstruck – ignorant of his next move. Should he risk waking the other children in the dormitory by going in or should he stay and risk getting caught. He got a fright. His heart started pounding into his throat. Panic. Tears have already begun to assemble in his eyes, but he couldn't cry, he needed to stay resilient – there were too much at stake. Yet the reality prevailed, he was exposed from both ends of the hallway – he had nowhere to go.

"Don't put on the lights," he whispered to himself. "Don't put on the lights." The darkness, his salvation. He beseeched his once childhood phobia to prevail in the awe time that surrounded him – to be his saviour.

Fortunately, it was. The room was not put to light, yet the voices got louder and louder with every passing second, up to a point where Arné could tell them apart. Three voices were whispering. And for a moment he allowed himself to eavesdrop on their conversation.

"And are you sure the ring is with him?" the one voice said.

"I can assure you it is. By tomorrow evening it will be in your possession," another voice said.

"Good," the last one said.

Arné suspended his lessor commission, realising that he had to make a plan. And fast. For if he couldn't think of something quickly enough, they would seize not only his attempt to get out of the house alongside Saturn but also his grand master plan to persevere. Every passing second felt like a waste of time. Who knows what they'll do to him if they found him out of bed at this hour? Suddenly he felt a hand coming from behind him reaching over his mouth. *This was it*, Arné thought, he was caught. Solitary again. That is if they haven't found a worse punishment for him yet. The hand dragged him into the dormitory by his side, and the next thing that he recognised, was soft cotton bedcovers covering his body. He kept silent. The hail of the three voices passed the dormitory slowly. Arné pulled the covers off himself.

"Sats," he whispered loudly. "It was you?" He thought it a miracle.

"Shh!" Saturn said, placing a finger on Arné's lips and browsing the room, "you're going to wake the others."

Arné started to breathe normally again. He was relieved to see that face. "I thought that you were asleep."

"I was," said Saturn. "Until you woke me, and I heard the voices."

"I didn't think I did."

"Well, you did," Saturn said rather irritably. "And why are you up at this hour? I thought that you were tired. You know that the staff do their rounds at this time. You could've gotten caught."

"I wanted to show you something," said Arné.

"No!" Saturn said a bit too loud.

"Shh!"

"We already went two times this week," Saturn tried to explain and yawned.

"Yeah, and so?"

"It's only the third day of the week," said Saturn.

Arné looked around to see if they had woken any of the other children. "Please," he begged as he looked back towards Saturn. "I have something I need to show you."

Saturn sighed and thought for a moment. "Okay," Saturn said with rolling eyes. "But it better not be stupid."

Saturn lent Arné a set of shoes as he had forgotten his own, and they didn't think it fit to return to his dorm to get them. And after they both had put them on, they bolted off. Silence could speak as well, and it spoke to Arné in a voice as clear as daylight: "Run!" it said, "run, for your lives depend on it." Thus, it was, with pounding hearts, and tipping shoes, and grasping hands, and flapping robes, Arné led Saturn through the hallways and staircases of the house, stopping at every corner, ensuring the coast clear before they continued on. The upshot of adrenaline rush from the actuality that they could get caught at any given moment could easily have been mistaken with fun – though it was nothing close to amusement.

"We better not get caught," Saturn whispered out of breath following Arné's footsteps, "again."

Saturn had good reason to feel and talk that way. Arné knew that. They had been caught once before; the punishment as a consequence was brutal. And although the house felt bigger tonight for some unknown reason, Arné stayed smoothly on course for Saturn's sake.

"Don't worry about it," he said with his head fixed afront, though as if there was a wall to his back and only one place to go. "We won't," he spoke with a sense of uncertainty. *Hopefully not*, he thought, *please, God, help us.* He felt lost, emotionally, and physically. His bearings unchecked, emotions running wild, though as if they were moving around in circles. But he kept confident, telling himself that no-one knew this house better than he did. He had done this with Saturn too many times not to know his way. They moved swiftly. And every time they would hear the slightest of a break-in silence, they would freeze for a moment, looking around to see if anybody was coming, and then continue. "We're almost there," Arné whispered with a sense of relief. "Just a few more steps and out the door we go." A few more steps they took, and unexpectedly, greeted by voices coming from the end of the last hallway. "Shh," Arné said.

"Oh my! Arné," Saturn said nervously. "If we get caught…"

"We won't," Arné replied quickly. "Well, at least not now," he tried to be sarcastic, but it was a pun that didn't make him feel as reassured as he wanted to, nor was it a joke that fit Saturn in the slightest of ways.

The voices luckily passed the hallway into another, and the two children were safe. It started to smell like cooked food, and the aroma was soon followed with the sight of kitchenware. It brought a discernment of closure to Saturn's senses. *Finally*, thought Saturn.

They always went out through the kitchen's back door; it was the most lenient way out. But going through the kitchen was the least complicated part of their journey. The kitchen staff were the meanest of them all. Feeding the children (in their own opinion) what tasted like dog food. And don't even think about complaining about it or asking for more, for here they would ground you just for that. There was no official plan. Only, when the coast was clear, you run for cover out the back door of the house. Simple you might think but more challenging than it seemed. Saturn was the first to go. And after Saturn, it was Arné's turn to run for it. His feet scooted over the floor beneath them. He was halfway there—just a few more steps. And only as he had reached the door, an unexpected hand grabbed him from behind. It pulled him back by his shirt's collar.

"And just where do you think you're going?" a voice accompanied the hand. It was the most infamous of the kitchen staff, the cook.

"I was only hungry," Arné quickly uttered addressing him as 'Sir'. Always addressing him as 'Sir'. "I wish for nothing but a little bit more please, Sir."

But the cook had nothing of it. "You know the rules," he said. "No more than what is needed," (*we don't even get that much*, Arné thought) he spoke pronouncing every syllable. He grabbed Arné by the ears and dragged him from the kitchen in that fashion. "You know the penalties for this type of behaviour."

Arné quickly glanced back just before they had exited the kitchen. "I'm on my way," he lip-talked to Saturn. "Wait for me."

They cook, dragging Arné by the ear, went straight to the principal's office. They entered after passing the secretary's joining office. The smell of cigar smoke in the air made Arné's nose itchy. There were wooden cabinets all around the room with each their own appropriate items showcased. Principal Malin, reading a newspaper, was sitting behind his old wooden desk in the middle of the room.

"I found this one snooping around in the kitchen," said the cook. "What ought I do to him?"

Principal Malin put down both what he was reading and his cigar in the ashtray and continued by looking at Arné, though as if he was an animal. "Again. Ai!" said Principal Malin.

"I was only looking for some food," Arné uttered before any other accusations could have been made against him – always addressing him as 'Sir'. Still, 'Sir.'

"Sure, you were…" Principal Malin said. "You know what I think. I think you tried to sneak out again. And as you know, we have a strangely special place for those who snoop and sneak where they shouldn't. Solitary!"

"Shall I take him?" asked the cook.

Eager to continue his reading, Principal Malin replied, "Yes."

The cook took Arné down to the basement where he locked him in one of the four wall-enclosed dungeon cells with only one small broken window giving light and air. The glint of moonlight shining in through the broken windowpane was like hope. Something was waiting on the other side.

Meanwhile, Saturn did as Arné had asked. Waiting outside in the cold breeze, imagining all the horrid things that might have happened to him. The draft shook the leaves of a couple of trees near the house. It didn't make Saturn feel more tranquil. And after about a quarter of an hour, Saturn thought that Arné was not going to come. Suddenly footsteps from behind, near the trees, approached Saturn in the dark. Saturn turned around. It was covered in dirt and moved slowly like a sinister shadow. Its feet pressed hard against the ground beneath them; like a beast trotting towards its prey.

Frightened, Saturn's heart pounded harder than the trotting of the shadow. "Who are you?" uttered Saturn.

"Saturn," said Arné. "It's me."

Saturn breathed Arné's name with relieve. "What happened?"

"Does it matter? I'm here now," said Arné. "Let's go." He grabbed Saturn's one hand while holding his journal in the other; together, the two – like shades – disappeared into the darkness of the morning-night, not looking back for one single moment. They were out, which was all that counted.

Chapter Ten

―――

A Search for Knowledge

ALL I EVER WANTED IN life was to know the truth; and if you had asked me some time ago, I would have told you, that was all I ever cared for. But that has changed along with my age. I was twenty-nine now, and I didn't care much for the truth anymore; these days, all I ever wanted in life was to have a story—any story. Yet, I couldn't avert from the truth; everything I needed and wanted to know, was here right in front of me, though obscured behind a sealed tongue.

Miss Hope's Alzheimer's, the barricade; separating ignorance from knowledge. And although I've counted the days since it had happened, I couldn't remember the last time she had recalled my name. As it was, it had happened about one week after my high school graduation: the one moment she tells me she is going out to do some grocery shopping, and the next moment I was called by a hospital. She was wandering around a few blocks away from our local shopping centre where she was lying face down on a sidewalk. The man who had found her described the event as seeing a drunk elderly woman, only to realise that that was not the case when he got to her. She was but only disoriented and dehydrated. As it turned out, she had hidden the symptoms from me for years. I know that now. And although it might sound unusual, I like to think of it as something heroic: she had done so to protect me. Due to that fact, I have never missed a day's appointment to come and visit her. She was there for me, and I'll be here for her.

Coming right from work, a nurse from the nursing home escorted me to her room. A gentle breeze blew a floral aroma from the garden; it blew in through columns supporting a canopy roof which separated apartment-style buildings. Hers was third from the entrance. As we passed the others, I couldn't prevent myself from peeking into those doors that stood ajar. I didn't want to come across as impolite, nor did I want anybody else to feel like I was invading their privacy. I was only curious to comprehend the facts, with a preparatory goal in mind, though I sometimes imagined their stories. We stopped. Miss Hope's door was closed, unlike all the others.

The nurse knocked and opened the door, speaking as she entered. "Hope," she said calmly. "There's someone here to see you. How are you feeling today?"

It befell me by shock every time I entered her room. I hated to see her this way. She was though a newborn stuck in a decaying body with no select fate of growing up. And although I had my hopes up every time, I had come to pay a visit, there wasn't any sign of progress.

"Hello, Miss Hope," I said. "It's me, Saturn."

She was seated in her sofa chair, staring out of her window with a garden view. I didn't think she noticed me – not even in the slightest – less even mentioning the recognition of my name. The nurse left, touching my shoulder in progress; she smiled with a quick glance as she passed me. Next to Miss Hope, the available armrest chair was soft and comfortable as I went over to sit on it.

"How have you been?" I asked, as I always did. And although I wouldn't still get a response, I would continue the conversation in any direction I saw proper. I had also observed the garden through the windowpane for a moment before I proceeded. "I'm doing good." I searched my mind for another subject to turnabout. "I think that I have already told you this, but I met my brother." (I have reported the account to her many times over, as it was. And though I made it sound like we've met recently; we had met a couple of years ago.) "His name's Jupiter," I continued excitingly. "A surprisingly good man, in my own opinion. I'm staying with him at the moment. Well, for at least a couple of years now, to be honest—him, his wife, and their baby girl. They are a lovely family, to say the least. And I love staying with them." I paused for a moment, reflecting on what else I could say. "Work is good. It's going well," I said. "I still enjoy giving piano lessons."

Her head moved, and it frightened me when she turned to look at me. For what I saw, was the blank expression of nothingness – no emotion whatsoever; I knew she didn't talk much anymore, but still, I couldn't get over those empty stares from her eyes. I went out to repose with some fresh air, and when I returned, I brought some sweet tea back with me. I helped Miss Hope to drink hers, though she was more than capable of doing it herself. I just cherished to feel close to her.

"Do you remember how we used to drink tea just like this? We used to do it all the time," I said.

And all of a sudden, she looked at me like she knew I was talking to her.

Although I knew these occurrences didn't last long, it gave me a sense of hope. "Are you the nurse?" she asked, confused. "No," I said. "I'm Saturn. Don't you remember? Saturn from the orphanage house."

She remained quiet for a moment. "Saturn is a planet, correct?" she said and turned back into a confused state.

I smiled. "Yes." I gently laughed. "It is a planet," I grinned at her. I loved it when she would speak to me. Although it didn't make sense all the time, I cherished it. "Do you remember the orphanage house?" I asked. "Sometimes, when I think back, I can't help but think that something is missing. Something is forgotten. Something – I'm even sometimes afraid of learning – that there might be something kept hidden from me. Something obscure." Every word I spoke was the truth. Till this day I don't know why I haven't talked to her about the orphanage house sooner, all those years back. But it didn't help to regret it now. What transpired was.

I heard a sudden knock on the door. It was the nurse. "Sorry, Saturn," she said. "I'm afraid that it's getting a bit too late and visiting hours will be over soon."

"That's okay, I understand," I told the nurse, and just before I left, I took Miss Hope's hand gently in mine so that she wouldn't get startled. "I miss you, you know that," I said with almost tears in my eyes. "I'll come back tomorrow again. See you soon and have a good night."

She replied with a blank expression turning to face the window again.

A cold, dry wind hit me in the face as I stepped from the apartment. It suggested dawn, just like the sight of darkness in the even-sky. I walked straight to the foyer, greeted the nurses on my way out, and called a cab.

Chapter Eleven

———

Plenty and Wealth

L IFE HAS, IN A WAY, taught me how to remain calm within the chaos, but nothing could have prepared me for this: I was cached to benightedness, and it didn't seem like enlightenment was coming my way any time soon. And although I'd have to admit it myself—my life has been instead a series of chronological scenes. That is, from my own accumulation of knowledge, and which had, of course, its slight natural variations here and there that set it apart from the norm – I couldn't put the thought of what had happened before Miss Hope, and I had come this way to rest.

Explanatorily – though I did not hold much knowledge of its particularities – my upbringing had consisted of three significant segments if you would analyse it from the perception of some grand design. The first origins; it had ensued beside my parents. As it was, from my mother, Celest, being an astrologer, and my father, Haven, being a jeweller, I was the second born; three years after my brother, Jupiter. And although I knew of them only what my brother had told me (which weren't much, as he too had come to lose them at an early age), I couldn't help myself but to apprehend that the accounts were always of the highest qualities. They gave me the impression of a more childish standard than a mature interpretation. But I still enjoyed listening to his stories as there weren't any pictures to showcase what our childhood was really like—all but one. The rest were lost, adjacent to some many other essential documents.

"Mother had the fairest red hair, short cut, and the most dazzling blue eyes," he once told me. "She was a bit on the chubby side, but it was all the size of love," he'd smile. "Father, on the other side, was the direct opposite. A serious man. He worked hard for a living, and he had it really, bad growing up too. He didn't have the most supportive of parents, you see. Neither did they have any money. So, education wasn't an option for him, you see. He had to work hard to get where he had ultimately ended up. He was a handsome man too, though he was still a bit on the skinny side, which complemented his hard indefatigable trait well. I could see why mom married him. He had dark hair and brown eyes."

The stories would idle indirectly within the background of our engagements, telling me now and then of their personalities and our experiences. How gentle they were towards each other, towards us; though Dad was a bit authoritarian ("go figure since his childhood"). Vacations ("always camping – since Dad's strong opinion towards the teachings of life") were still amusing.

Consequently, losing my parents, and eventually, my brother was the second segment of my upbringing. I had therefore spent these years of my life in an orphanage house. But of it, I had no account.

And thus, had arrived the final division of my accountable life that I spent with Miss Hope. At its dawn, unconsciousness. And only by a sting on my right arm had I awoke from it. The stiffness around my entire body paralysed me, enough so that I was incapable of bringing my left hand up to feel what had caused the prick. Divergently, my damp and heavy eyes emulated my tongue like a sponge craving for anything to quench my thirst.

"Hello, Dearie. How are we feeling?" a voice echoed into my half-closed ears that worsened my head beating against its own wall.

The blurry scene confused me, as all I could secure from the view was a white overcoat. The sensation had not let go of me for at least an hour or two (or at least that was what it felt like), and by the time I regained some consciousness, all it could interpret of my senses was four individuals standing with solicitude right in front of my hospital bed. After the explanations and some more interpretation, they identified as Miss Hope, a doctor, a nurse, and a woman dressed formally, who I had found out later was a social worker. The sequence of events after that still occurred obscured through a dark lens as I still needed to make sense of the mess regarding the order in which they had presented itself to me. Frankly, of which I, till this day, can't.

However, I remember the doctor and his nurse being kind as he greeted me. The social worker warm-heartedly explained what had happened and what needs to happen now; Miss Hope lovingly, like a genuine parent's intent, stayed by my side – all during which they gave me something to eat and drink. As it was, a fire had broken out and ultimately ruined the orphanage house where I resided. Fortunately, there wasn't a single burn mark located on the side of my body. Unfortunately, as we had soon discovered that day, the same major blow to my head that had left me unconscious during the fire had also left me memoryless.

Nevertheless, that too passed, and the years which followed that day I had come to live with Miss Hope. It was a considerable healthy and enjoyable life. High school was fulfilling, though I hadn't many friends, and for the most part, my best accountancy was the piano. Music had impressed me insofar that after graduation, I enrolled for a degree in music at university and finished after four years. This conclusively resulted in the life of a music teacher I endured now.

The three segments that I cherished insofar, for they were the only knowledge I possessed, demonstrating my life's accuracy, however, was not much the individual events that had come to haunt me so. It was those two nebulous disasters which had occurred to separate them, which had held the concealment of obscurity and shameful secrets of my life. Their significance had arisen from their indifference. The separators: losing my parents, and the mysterious night at the orphanage house that had caused my amnesia.

These were the mares that occupied my mind outside the nursing home where a gentle and cold breeze that suddenly transmuted into a rainstorm pulled me from my thoughts. It acquired me to run to the nearest shelter I could find. And tightening my jacket around my waist, I shivered through the wait under the bus stop shelter located near the nursing home. The headlights of the taxicab approached me through the mist of the rain a couple of minutes later. After it pulled over, I climbed in. And with an unwilling feeling of putting the day to rest and go home, I gave the cabdriver instruction to take me to the botanical garden. I needed to clear my head.

Chapter Twelve

―――――

Generation

INTIMACY IN THE FORM OF love. Life has not presented me much of this, so I took hold of it with gratitude when and if life did. However, I couldn't help myself but feel a slight sense of suspicion resulting in a particular unconscious caution every time it did happen. I'd always consult life's cruelty from previous times and debate over why it would come to treat me better now. What chance did I genuinely have that the odds were indeed in my favour? This is why, when I met Jupiter some years ago, I reacted the way I did.

As it was, we coincided again, after we were dissentfully split-up in our adolescence, one late evening when I was twenty-five. It was around the time when I finished my music degree and started to work at the music conservatorium as a piano teacher for beginners. A gentle even-breeze accompanied me on my walk from the bus stop which was located a few houses away, towards the suburban home where Miss Hope and I had lived in together before she went to the nursing home. I had come from Miss Hope when I got to the front porch and found a strange man sitting on my doorstep. He was dressed casually in jeans and a t-shirt.

Nevertheless, our unacquaintance didn't prevent me from approaching him. As I got closer to him, his appearance became more familiar to me. It enlightened against the unfamiliarity of our acquaintanceship. He was handsomely built with evenly as attractive facial features. His beard, trimmed across his strong jawline, had the same deep brown colour – almost black – just like his short-cut hairstyle fashioned with wax. Yet, I was frightened. I still didn't recognise him from anywhere. But the neighbour's lights were still on, and their speech gave me a sense of reassurance that if something odd to happen, they'll be able to hear me scream or apprehend some form of violence going on outside.

"Hello, can I help you?" I said.

He sprung up as soon as he noticed me and dusted off his jeans in the process. "Hello," he uttered, though as if he was out of breath. He didn't appear to be violent. "Saturn," he said. The tone made it challenging to distinguish his discourse from being vocative or curious and questioningly. Yet, it was emotional for him to pronounce my name. I could see that; his deep brown eyes impersonated a lament. It was the opposite of my own reaction, though. He knew my name, and I did not know his.

I looked at him suspiciously. "Yes…" I said.

He hesitated. And for a brief moment, we observed at each other without the judgement of words.

"I—" he started, "I am your—" he paused though as if he was looking for the right word. Though as if he knew what he wanted to say but struggled to say it, "…brother," he said. It was straight forward, and for a moment, it almost seemed like he moved slightly on though, as if he wanted to give me a hug.

I took a step back with my hand up. I didn't reply. Yet I thought, *is this some form of a sick joke?*

"Now, I know this might be too much," he started. "But my name is Jupiter," he continued. "And I was just as surprised as you were when I had found out that you were still alive," he continued some more. His words were articulated, though as if he wanted to calm me, albeit the more he spoke, the more sombre it made me. "I'm so happy to see you again after all these years," he said again and approached me with open arms.

But I quickly ran up the porch. "Get out! Get out of my face!" I said.

"What do you mean?" he said. "Don't you remember me?" He was confused; he didn't know what had happened to me.

The keys rattled in my hand as I unlocked the front door.

"I know you have a ring," he said. I was about to enter the house, slamming the door behind me, when his words halted me by the frame. "Of shimmering pinks, hues of grey and a hint of brown—"

I threw myself around. "Listen to me," I said. "I don't know who you are, or where you come from, or how you know about my ring, or how you know my name. But if you ever come about a mile's radius from me ever again, I swear I'll call the police."

He didn't listen, of course, and I didn't call the police on him; I'd hoped that he would go away by himself. But I found him again the following morning, waiting outside my house.

"Please just listen to me," he'd say. "I'm telling the truth," he'd continue.

"Haven't I made myself clear?" I'd say, shutting him down every time. And every night I'd lay in bed querying over it. *Could it be true? Could I have a brother?* But it was excessively farfetched. If it was true, why didn't Miss Hope mention him ever, and where was he all this time? Yet, I couldn't avert the sentiment of emotion every time I did see him. For what I saw was confusion worse than mine every time I didn't recognise him.

It continued for about a week where I'd found him in the same manner, either in the early morning or in the evenings after work upon my return from Miss Hope. That is, until one night I decided to call the police on him. The phone rang in my ear as I peered through my kitchen window, my eyes never leaving his sight. I've had about enough of it frankly. Yet, I couldn't help but pity him; a particular type of sadness surrounded his air.

"Hello, Central Police Station," an officer answered the line. "How can we assist you?"

And just as I wanted to begin my rant. Astonishment! A child ran up to the once stranger of my view. I would've guessed her around the age of three (as I learned later, she was). Still plump of baby fat, she moved slowly towards Jupiter as her brown hair followed. From inside, their converse was a mystery to my ears; outside, their attitudes reflected sharply, simulating the sun's warmness. Once the child had reached him, he picked her up. He started to walk forwards as he did. Amazed, I stared on. For my gaze too fixed on him and the child, blinded me to see the woman towards whom he walked. She echoed the same description than that of the child, only slightly leaner. *It must be his wife*, I thought. *And maybe, the child was theirs.* It got me by surprise. He seemed a family man. Charming too. And the child and woman's comfort around him revealed him well.

"Hello? Is everything alright," said the officer.

The sight of them had me completely forget about the officer on the other side of the phone. "Hello," I said calmly. "Yes, everything is fine. My child called the number by accident. I apologise, officer," I lied of course so that he wouldn't call me back.

"That's okay. It happens. You have a lovely evening."

I responded in reverence, "Thank you, Officer, you too," and put the phone down, and then rushed outside as quickly as I possibly could before they left. I didn't know what to say, but the front door shutting behind me as I exited, caught the family's attention. We all stared at each other for a moment. "Do you want to come in?" I asked timidly and straightforward.

He glanced towards the woman. She nodded. "We'd love to," he said.

Inside, a few minutes after introductions and pleasantries, I found myself talking to Jupiter in the kitchen. Jupiter and I were making us some hot drinks while Serenity (which was the name of the woman and also Jupiter's wife) sat and played with Happiness, their lovely baby girl, in the living room.

"I would like to apologise for my behaviour again," I said. "Please understand that it's not every day that—" I struggled to find the words.

"That's okay," Jupiter intervened politely and stayed very calm. "I understand. Honestly, I didn't know how to approach you. After I found out that you were still alive, I only wanted to see it for myself. I was a bit overwhelmed, to be honest."

"What do you mean by that?"

"By what?"

"When you say that when you found out that I am still alive?" I asked curiously.

"Well, it was all over the news," he said. "That a child had died at that orphanage house."

"I see."

"I thought it was you…"

I didn't give him a chance to pronounce the last syllable. "Why?" I asked curiously.

And all of a sudden, he looked heartbroken.

"I apologise if I—"

"No, it's not that," he said. "It's the same reason why I know that you have a ring. And it's the link between that ring and mom and dad because we had the lives we had. That's why I thought so."

"I do not understand," I spoke with confusion.

"You really do not remember anything, do you?"

I shook my head speechlessly. I didn't know what he was talking about.

"Mom and Dad were murdered for that ring, Saturn," he spoke informatively yet melancholically. "It is the reason why they are dead. The thieves and murderers never got it, of course. They were caught, red-handed by the police, standing over our parents' bodies. And the next thing you know, we were shipped off to an orphanage house in the middle of nowhere. The police spread some rumour that the ring was stolen and never found. It was, of course, a diversion, a distraction from us. But the ring had remained in my possession until one day when I was shipped off—" he kept still for a while, and I could hear how he struggled to speak; he continued pensively, "off to a juvenile detention centre, I gave it to

Miss Hope to pass it down to you. But I thought that somebody had found out about them and went to steal it. Taking whatever life necessary if one stood in their way."

I didn't have the ring he was talking about anymore. Yet I knew of it as Miss Hope had one day in her lucidness, asked me about it. But it was gone. Maybe even stolen. Yet I was curious to know why he felt like he was my brother. And, I felt itchy around my chest area, though as if it longed for something hanging from around my neck. Till this day I never told him that the ring was gone. Lost. Stolen, maybe. And fortunately, he had never demanded, nor ever showed any intend for me to show it to him, which was one of the reasons I felt safe with him. He remained calm although still in distress. He had me suspicious too, frankly. If what he said was true, how did I not know that he wasn't after it himself? And that the woman and child were just a diversion. But before I was too quick to judge and made any such conclusions, I asked, "And how did you find me?"

"I saw a picture of you and Miss Hope in the conservatory. One evening when we went to see a show."

I could see from the look in his eyes that he knew he hadn't me convinced. That was when he pulled out one single photo from his pocket; it wasn't until he had done so that I had come to believe him. It was a photo of him and I. "It was taken in front of the orphanage house days before they shipped me off," he said. "You honestly don't remember any of it?"

I shook my head slightly as I looked upon his face. I was starting to believe him.

"I gave the ring to Miss Hope the evening before it happened. The evening before they took me away. I asked her to give it to you. And the day when we were dragged from each other, I promised you that I'll one day return. That I'd one day come back for you. I never forgot that promise." He sounded convincing and decent. He knew Miss Hope too, describing her in exact detail, he knew so much I didn't. And still, he didn't ask me to see the ring.

The days that followed, we shared each other's stories over either lunch or dinner. I told Jupiter mine (that which I knew, of course). He shared his own. How after juvie he became an engineer and how he and Serenity, met at university. He told me everything I, today, knew of our parents. I was lucky to re-meet him. I assume that something like this doesn't happen very often. And a few months later, I moved into his and Serinity's suburban home and where I participated in and enjoyed the quiet-outer life. So, I always portrayed my gratitude. And when and if I found him cooking for the family, or doing something beneficial for them, I thought how blessed I was to have him in my life. I had come to trust him with comfort, just like I did with Miss Hope.

Inside, sitting aback of the taxicab, the windows started to fog-up as I regarded the botanical garden entrance. The trip flew by just like the rainstorm which occurred with it. My right hand, pressed against my upper chest where I thought the ring once hung from around my neck, came down to open the door as we pulled over. I paid the cab driver and climbed out. Bearing the thought of the ring in mind, I entered the garden, undressed my shoes, and started to walk around. Not even Jupiter knew the origins of the ring. Though he knew the name: Saturn's Rings. Where did it come from? How had our parents ultimately come to own it? It was all still a mystery. And sometimes I couldn't help myself but wonder if it was real. Or was it just a made-up tale?

Something I had come to believe in for years. After Jupiter had told me all about it, I have searched my mind for even the slightest of detailed memories about it, but I never succeeded at recalling anything. Never. And yet, within all the detailed accounts he had given me about it, it felt familiar. However, still, I couldn't help but feel a missing piece about it as well—something about it that was still unspoken.

Chapter Thirteen

———

Periodical Renewal

IT WAS THOUGH AS IF I saw daylight within the night. For as my eyes feasted upon him, my mind had presented me with a glimpse into my unknown past. A memory. A young boy with dark-brown hair who took my hand and ran with it underneath a big tree. There was the orphanage house too, with some hills, and a mountain and a lake; all within the landscape. A ring hanging around my neck substantiated Jupiter's story. And although he was much older now, I was sure of it. That he was the one within the memory.

So, I, at that moment, forgot the actual reason why I had come to the botanical garden in the first place. I was indulged in contemplating a man's image in front of the wall and the two trees. Before I did, I had wondered about the garden barefoot. I loved the feeling of raw nature underneath my feet, and it brought me an enormous amount of joy to break this one social convention being perceived as madness. I had searched for what my eyes could not see. And yet when I saw him, I knew that I had found it.

The man looked haunted, though, and I at once felt a considerable amount of sympathy towards him. Whatever he was thinking about, I felt like I could relate. I have been changed as well during my life. I have heard about the exact colours in the worst of men. How it had affected me without any knowledge of it, and it had also brought a vast amount of sorrow into my life, but I have entrusted myself with a vow to stay positive; that I shall not let the mal doings of others reduce me. There was something off about his appearance though. For although he looked haunted, he seemed very well-adjusted too. But I convinced myself of other things: *maybe it was money*, I thought. *Perhaps life got him down a bit, and something didn't work out, or probably, it was of simpler things*. Nevertheless, the joyful scream of a little girl made me even more suspicious.

"Papa!" she shouted.

The intend of great love was well-conveyed by the tenderness in her voice as she approached the man – her father, I assumed. Her little legs carried her one after the other over the grassland that laid between them. Her light brown hair, following her, brushed through the wind. The innovation from the ill mood was inspiring. The man reached out to catch her, and as he did, he spun around and carefully cast her up into the air. Her laughter echoed into my ears as he grabbed her again. He smiled. Thereupon, the girl presented him with lavender. And although I could see their lips moving, I couldn't make out what they were speaking about, but it looked cheerful. The child was rather quickly distracted after that. She squirmed from his grip and dashed towards a boy, around the age of ten, standing a few meters away from them. The comfort around the man and the children made me trust in the feeling that they were family.

My feet started to hurt. It has been a long day, so I decided to sit on a bench, not more than a couple of meters away from where I stood. My apprehension about being caught by them made me try and do it stealthily, though it wasn't a public space, and I weren't supposed to be here. And although I could, I didn't want to interrupt. The cold grass tickled my bare feet as I kept my eyes on the man. A terrible mistake, I soon realised as the crack of a stick underneath my one foot sounded an alarm. I should have looked to the ground instead. They heard my heavy tread, and it unveiled my presence.

"Papa!" the girl said. "Look!"

The little girl's recognition of my presence collaborated with a quick glance from the boy towards my way.

"I see," the man said though as if he already knew I was there. And he spoke softly too, though as if he wanted to calm the girl.

I felt like prey within that moment as the man looked my way. Seconds passed like hours as he looked at me with big, wide eyes though as if he knew me. I didn't know what to do, so I waved and smiled like an idiot. *I wonder what he must be thinking*, I thought. *Stalker person maybe*. He glanced towards the little girl and then back towards me. It was difficult. He didn't even twitch; nothing also indicating a smile. The girl dashed back towards him and hid behind his legs.

"Go to your brother, Chris," he said, all with a change of tone.

But like any other child her age would do at times, she disobeyed. She did the exact opposite of what the man had asked of her. She came to me instead. She stopped swiftly by my side and smiled as her hands were held behind her back. She glanced towards her father and then peered back at me though I was familiar to her sight. Her hands came from behind her, and she gently showed me the lavender she had shown her father earlier. I went down on my one knee and smelled the lavender scent.

"Lavender," I said. "That's my favourite." And as I tried to take the flower from her hand, she pointed it towards her father.

"Papa's too," she said.

The man suddenly walked our way. With every step he took, my eyes grew wider. And as he reached us, he too went down on one of his knees. The girl smiled as she placed the flower in his hand and gently pressing it towards me. Preceding the butterflies, my heart pounded blood towards my face, while he looked calm, though as if nothing had happened. *Was it me?* I thought. I think it might have been me. But I tried to convince myself that it wasn't. However, I took the lavender carefully, not touching either of them in the process. Then I lifted myself from the ground.

"I have to go," I said with a little bit of breath the experience had left me with. My feelings were the antithesis of my speech. I didn't want to go. For what I perceived when I saw the man was prosperity, a certain kind of disclosure. He was in a memory I had gotten. It would have been foolish of me to leave now, and not regard what the night might traverse.

The girl went back to her brother as the man suddenly spoke with a face turning pale, though as if he had seen a ghost.

"No, don't!" he said. "Stay! I mean, please. I don't want to be alone."

I didn't know what to think of it. Why on earth would he say that he doesn't want to be alone? After all, I was the one who was alone, not him. "Okay," I said hesitatingly.

We moved towards the bench where we sat awkwardly, not exchanging another word. The man lit himself a cigarette and began to smoke it. When he had finished it, he went to throw the butt away and came right back. I looked at him, and I looked at the children and curious to find out when I brought my wrist up. It was almost midnight. And as I looked back up, they were nowhere to be found within my sight.

"Where are they?" I asked disturbingly. And with a glance towards the man after I had spoken, I was stunned. My glance quickly turned into reverence. I got a fright. For what I heeded was mutation: the same man who sat next to me resembled himself at least ten years younger than before—a nonsensical observation.

Yet, the imminent apex of the night approached us as he looked at me with a profound sense of tone and emotion. "Gone," he cried.

Chapter Fourteen

Liberation

THE ABSENCE OF HIS VIEW from my sight left me blind; I yearned to see the face of the man I met in the garden.

The following day, with reason, I fell subject to the habit of the date: wake-up, work, Miss Hope. When I finally got to the garden, with the anticipation of seeing him again, I rummaged the range of the plot for him with the eyes of a hawk. Within the plain sight of the area. Behind every bush and tree. Up the small hills, and down the rivulet. But he was nowhere to be found. I was at it for about an hour, my feet consequently started to hurt – it was a long day too – and I wanted to sit down for a while. So, I decided to sit on that same bench where he and I had sat yesterday evening in ponderous secrecy. I looked up. The stars glittered next to the moon without a sign of a single cloud in sight. I closed my eyes. And for a minute I allowed my feelings to have authority over my mind, thinking I was alone.

Last night had left me mute, as well, in many ways. Not only because we parted without any increase of verbal exchange, but also in a way that my unanswered questions had exceeded me. The solution—the sensation of senses: most notably, I needed to see him again. For my other stimuli, depending on the admission of my sight. Incidentally, though it might sound impossible, I felt an incredible feeling of fancy towards him, though as if it was a retainment thereof; that I couldn't avert the sentiment of thought that there was once a time I had cherished him. As it was, I haven't ever felt this way towards another person and always thought that I would grow old alone.

I opened my eyes and got a fright; I was not alone. Dressed in black, they looked at me with deep dark eyes; one standing to my right, and another a few meters away in front of me. They were the two strangest men I have ever beheld. They appeared though, like ghosts haunting me from my undiscovered antiquity.

I stood up. "I apologise," I said (hopefully the men only wanted to sit where I sat). "I thought that I was alone." I started to walk away.

My feet trotted against the gravel of the walkway like the pounding of my heart, and I began to pray for coincidence as I noticed the two strange men following me. It felt like a nightmare, though as if I was experiencing a fantasy of my yore. I kept the pace. By now, my eyes were screening the garden to see if anybody else was around. But to my adversity, no one was. I tried to ignore the inescapable, pretending like they weren't there, but the inevitable erupted. Suddenly, the harsh movements of hands covered my mouth while another pressed me against a chest. I tried to scream and squirm my way out of it, but I was in the vast clutch of one of the men, and it didn't seem like support was coming my way anytime soon. The other man shot to my front. He stood so close that I could almost feel him breathing on my face. My vision was blocked. Even if there was help, I wouldn't have been able to see it. I breathed heavily through my nose, trying to make up for all the oxygen my heart pounded through my veins. But I was smothered. Slowly and steadily suffocating to death.

Then, out of nowhere, like the sound of silence breaking before an apex, I heard the voice of a man calling in deliverance. "Sorry!" he shouted. "Are you okay down there?"

I felt relieved to my very bones. What were the chances?

"Hey— you!" he shouted again. "Is everything alright?" His voice got louder though as if he was heading our way.

The two strange men were disturbed by the alarm of the other man. A slight release and a new clutch of the man who was holding me from behind demonstrated hesitation. The man to my front showcased fear, haste, and interruption through his eyes.

"Arné?" the one behind me suddenly breathed into my ear.

"Ring!" the one in front of me said. "Where is the ring?" By the time he pronounced the last syllable the third man was closing in.

The walkway's hard gravel sanded my hands in the attempt to break my fall as the two strange men released me. They disappeared like ghosts into the night.

"Are you okay?" I suddenly heard next to me. The man sounded concerned as he gently assisted me up onto my feet again.

Shocked, I didn't pay any attention to his description. I didn't even look him in the eye. "Yes," I said out of breath, "I'm fine. Thank you." And much startled by the event without thinking twice, I started to walk away immediately, heading straight home.

The effects of the two preceding evenings left me insomnious that night. And the following morning, I caught Jupiter, downstairs in the kitchen cooking breakfast like he always did, by surprise.

"Up already," he said, "and ready for work already, I see." He looked stunned by my unusual habit.

"Good morning to you too," I grinned as I didn't know how else to respond and went on pouring myself a cup of coffee from the filter machine.

"Good morning." He laughed as he arranged the centre counter of the kitchen with the appropriate dishes. "I didn't hear you come in last night," he said concerningly, "late evenings at work?" It wasn't, in fact, an unexpected question. I came in late two nights in a row which was very rare for me.

I didn't respond. Jupiter's question made my thoughts occupy themselves with the episodes of the two preceding evenings, instead.

"Sats," he called. "Is everything alright?" He looked at me worryingly.

"Yeah," I startled back into the conversation. "Sorry, I just didn't sleep well."

"Is there something you want to talk about?"

"No, I'm fine. Just a lot at work." I lied, of course. I didn't want to bring it up, didn't want to talk about it. For in my mind, it was all still confusing. A mess. I couldn't make sense of it. "Sorry, I think I'm late for work. I must get going." I finished my coffee.

"That's okay," he said caringly leaving it there. "Have some breakfast before you go. Can't start a day without the proper breakfast."

The taste of eggs and bacon on my tongue was gratifying. Jupiter and I continued our conversation over other, more satisfying topics, less stressful than *work*. I finished up breakfast and left home before Serenity and Happiness could join us downstairs.

The year that followed that day, I fell into the habitual lifestyle of getting up, going to work, visiting Miss Hope, have a look at the botanical garden, going back home, spent some quality time with my brother and his family, going to bed. The following day everything would repeat itself. I never saw the man of my memory ever again, nor did I see the two strange men who assaulted me. Yet, quite frankly, though they had left me, I couldn't come to let go of them. And so it was that one evening sitting in front of Miss Hope, one year after repeatedly staring into those same empty eyes, I was suddenly overtaken by divulgence. To grab hold of something anew, I had to let go of that one thing I had once deemed my deliverance. I had to leave in order to find myself. So, I took Miss Hope's hand, and I apologised for the promise that I was about to break. And I went home, expressing my grief on the way, to speak to Jupiter. I caught him coming outside of Happiness's room, after laying her to sleep.

"Hi, Sats," he said, startled as we bumped into each other.

"Hi," I greeted back pensively.

"Everything okay?"

"Good," I said and paused. "Actually, not that great, I was wondering if we could talk?"

"Sure," he said concerningly. "Let's make ourselves a nice cup of tea."

We went downstairs to the kitchen where he put on the kettle and allowed it to boil.

"I remembered something," I said before he could ask me anything.

"Wow," he said. "That's great. How and when did it happen?"

I went on and told him the story of the man in the garden I had met. Leaving out the bits about his 'transformation' and the two strange men.

"Why didn't you ever tell me back then?"

"I didn't want to worry you. You have a lot on your own plate, and I didn't want to add to it. Plus, it didn't happen again. So, I left it there."

"Sats, you will never be too much of anything," he said lovingly.

"Thanks," I grinned. "But that wasn't what I wanted to talk to you about."

"Yes?" he said concerningly.

"I was thinking about leaving." I knew he wouldn't stop me. He wasn't my parent, and it wasn't like I was fifteen. Yet I felt like I owed him an explanation.

"Have you thought about where you're going?"

"Back," I said.

"Back where," he interrupted.

"To the orphanage house," I said. "Or, well, back to Old Town that is. I was thinking about the memories, and since it hadn't occurred again, I was thinking maybe if I go back, then maybe I would remember more."

"I see," he didn't sound convinced.

"If there's a chance that my memories might come back, I think the best place for it to happen would be the place where I had lost them."

"Saturn," he said, "are you sure this is what you want?"

"I am, Jupiter," I said. "I think this is what I need to do. To give up on what I thought I once knew and look for something new. To find me again."

Chapter Fifteen

———

A Sense of Knowledge

THE THIRTEEN-HOUR BUS RIDE felt like I had a backrow seat into my past, partially afraid of what I might uncover. Yet, within all the unfamiliarity, a sense of knowledge arose stealthily. And though the trip cleared my mind of any unwanted thoughts, the start thereof had unveiled a nostalgic reaction. For what I felt was longing, a type of sadness for leaving – that I could have, if I wanted to, stayed. But I had to let go. I had to leave some things behind for me to learn and grow.

The bus came to a standstill, and I watched the passengers find the exit. I waited for a while. Then it struck me. I was alone for the first time ever since I could remember. And though my eyes were heavy, the adrenalin generated from the former thought, pressed me. I climbed out of the bus. The sun was already busy setting, on this first day I arrived, and I quickly had to rush to the nearest hotel to book myself a room for the night. I was surprised to see how unorganised I was; I didn't think this entirely through. Nevertheless, with my suitcase in hand, I raced to the nearest hotel I could find and booked myself a single bed for the night. And without any other further ado, I headed straight for bed without having anything for dinner.

I woke up the following morning, feeling lethargic. The bed swallowed me, and although I was hungry, I didn't feel like getting up. When I finally succeeded at pulling myself from the bed, I poured myself a big glass of water and thought about the things I had to do: apartment and work. The hotel was expensive, and I doubted that I would be able to stay here for the entire week, or even three nights. That motivated me. I pulled myself together and got out.

It was a small town and looked rather like a village, in my opinion – something representing a European settlement. I did some window shopping as I passed all the cute little stores and went into a small coffee shop where I had thought to get some breakfast. The doorbell rang as I entered through the door, and a short, old woman with long red hair greeted me directly after that with much hospitality. Her nametag read "Patience."

"Table for one, Honey?" she asked.

"Yes, please," I said with a smile.

She led me to a window seat. "I'll give you a few minutes to decide," she said, leaving a menu as she walked away.

I chose the least expensive thing on the menu; I didn't know how long I would survive with the money I had. After that, my head turned, and my eyes revered from the windowpane. I thought about the town, and although I couldn't remember anything thereof, I thought about how much it must have changed since I've been here.

"Decided on anything yet, Honey?" Patience returned.

My attention came back. "Yes," I said and pointed out on the menu what I wanted. "I'll have the coffee with the egg and bacon breakfast, please."

"Certainly," she said gently and took my menu. "Would that be all?"

"Yes," I replied.

As I waited for my order, I looked around the coffee shop. Surprise opened my eyes as I saw that the lady was the only one working in the house. That was, of course, apart from the old man who I saw working in the kitchen. When my meal arrived, I finished it as fast as it came and went straight to the till to pay my bill.

"Are you new in town, Honey?" Patience asked as she checked the register.

"Yes," I replied timidly as I got some courage to ask for something else.

"Well, you're going to love it here," she said. "Everyone is so nice here. You'll see."

I smiled. "Thank you," I said, and I took my loose change. "I'm sorry if this is too upfront, Ma'am," I uttered silently, "but I couldn't help but notice that you are the only one working here apart from the man in the kitchen. And I was, well wondering if you might need an extra set of hands. I will really appreciate it if I could maybe help?"

"Oh!" she grinned. "You can call me Patience, Honey. And how nice of you to offer." She was surprised to see me asking, but she must have seen how desperate I was. "Just wait for a second, I'll be back in just a minute," she said and disappeared through the kitchen door aback.

It was only a couple of seconds later when she returned with the man by her side. I stared with a pounding heart, embarrassed, desperate, and scared. The man was taller than he looked from a distance, and he had a fascinating look on his face. His boldness made him look tough, yet his face expressed a certain kind of tenderness. And within the awareness of his description, I felt something familiar about him. Yet, I couldn't place my finger on it.

He halted for a brief moment after he stepped through the kitchen door, though as if he recognised me. "I hear you're looking for a job?" he spoke with a deep, kind voice though as if he knew me.

I remained silent for a moment, still trying to figure out where I might know him from. "Yes," I said timidly. I didn't say anything else.

"A bit on the quiet side, I see. We'll have to work on that," the man grinned. "But we can most definitely do with an extra pair of hands around here," he said thoughtfully.

"Thank you, Sir, I really appreciate it. You will not regret it."

"You can call me Faith," he said kindly, and before he left, he added, "you can come tomorrow morning at six. We open at seven."

The following morning, I arrived not a minute over six o'clock and was ready to start my first day at work. They handed me attire and Patience showed me around the shop. The pressure of remembering everything she told made me forget about the stresses of starting a new job.

And just before we opened, Faith walked up to me with my name tag. "I forgot to ask your name," he said.

"Saturn, Si—" I almost addressed him incorrectly, "Faith."

"Saturn," he said pensively as his brown eyes stared into mine. "Saturn," he said again this time more seriously. "I'll get back to you with the tag," he said and disappeared.

A slightly awkward moment, in my own opinion. Yet, I felt like there were something more to it. But I didn't want to be too much, so I didn't nettle with it. Later that day, he returned politely, handed me my tag, and went straight back to work. The day went by quickly, and before I knew it, it was around eight that evening, and we closed the shop.

"Good day, Honey?" Patience asked as she checked the register for final admin check-ups.

"Some trouble with the orders but mostly good," I joked. It was, in fact, better than I had anticipated. Long hours, yes; but three meals were included.

Faith entered the conversation from the kitchen. "Oh, I won't worry too much about that. You'll learn the tricks to it quickly," he grinned.

They were the most loving couple (as I learned earlier that day, they have been married for just about over ten years now) I have ever met.

"Where are you staying at, Honey?" Patience asked. "Can we drop you off?"

"I'm actually staying at a hotel for the moment. Still need to get some place more permanent."

"Oh, well, there's some space upstairs," Faith said. "You could stay here if you want to."

"Oh!" Patience started, "what a fantastic idea. It is such a pity for such a room to remain abandoned."

They were very generous, and it was, at first, an awkward thought, but I agreed in the end. So, the following day, I found myself cleaning out the upper apartment for residency and moved in straight away. After about a week, I started to get the hang of how everything worked. And although nothing noticeable had come to pass concerning my original plans, I concentrated on the positive: I had a place to stay and food on the table. But that was about to change. It was lunchtime as I stood by the counter, fixing a coffee for one of the tables.

"Look," Patience said. "There he is again." She spoke to both her husband and myself.

I turned around to see who it was, but I only got a glimpse of his back.

"He comes here every Sunday afternoon," whispered Patience. "I'll leave you to it," she patted me on my shoulder.

He had taken himself a menu on his way in and went to sit on the same place I sat the first time I came to this café. I walked over to him to take his order. He looked calm from behind, and by the influence of Patience's speech, I sensed sadness too. I fiddled through my pocket for my notebook and turned to a blank page.

"Hello, and welcome to the coffee house," I said as I took out my notebook and pen. "Would you like anything to eat or to drink?" He lowered the menu showing his face as I looked up from my booklet. And there he sat. The man. The man from the garden. *What are the chances?*

Chapter Sixteen

Left Behind

Arné and Saturn had tried to leave that house behind them as many times as they had come to return to it. Yet that urge to escape it had never seized to evade from their existence. The moon hovered like a balloon by its string above the house. It was accompanied by one single cloud framing the stars in the night-time sky. The two children crossed the meadow's vegetation with the hills and mountain standing vast in the distance, yet not entirely visible.

"Come on, Sats!" Arné said as he looked back. He was leading the way, as he always does, now and then looking around to make sure that Saturn wasn't falling behind.

"I'm right behind you!" Saturn said out of breath.

They were walking for about half an hour now, and the grass of the meadow was slowly picking up hight. Dry sticks started to appear on the ground, and a gentle breeze blew through the long grass; they were well at the beginning of the grassland, and the marsh was just up ahead. Arné paused. His eyes explored the ground around himself.

Saturn caught up. "What are you doing?"

"Looking for a stick," Arné said as he bent down to pick one up. It was sufficiently long to be used as a cane and thick enough to remain intact when he cuts the long grass out of their way. He looked at Saturn. "This one might do—" he said.

Suddenly, a howl in the wind made him catch his breath. The two children stared at each other with wide eyes as a single bark after the wail had turned both of their faces pale.

"What was that?" Saturn said wobbly, knowing well the answer to that question.

"We forgot about the hound!" exclaimed Arné.

Another bark turned their stomachs upside down.

"What do we do?" cried Saturn.

"Run!" said Arné. "Run! We need to get to the marsh now!"

The two children dashed forwards through the long grass like two meerkats on a hunt. The barks of the dog got louder. It started to thunder behind them like a warning for a significant storm's advent. *Hound, hound, hound*, Arné's own blindness chastened himself. *Who in their right mind would have forgotten about the hound?* He always remembered to lock the dog's gate before they snuck out. Always.

"Arné," said Saturn.

"Just keep on going!" He said as he followed closely behind Saturn. "Faster!"

"I'm trying."

The long grass had grown, well the hight of their shoulders and they started to whip the children hastening through them, and small leaps over hillocks made them slow down their pace. The barks of the dog got louder. It was only a matter of time before the dog will catch up to them. Suddenly, a hard cracker sound booming in the air behind them made Saturn stumble and fall to the ground. Arné, in motion, passed Saturn a few meters and turned back the second he heard his name shouted. Arné hastened towards Saturn.

"He's shooting," cried Saturn. "Why would he shoot?"

"I don't know. The idiot must think that we're foxes or something."

The first time (also the time Arné had learned to lock the dog in) when it had happened, they merely heard shouts. This was the first time ever the watchman had followed his dog out into the field, shooting. Arné tried to pick Saturn up, but suddenly, out of nowhere, the dog jumped them. It snatched Saturn by the leg; fortunately, only scraping the tissue and holding on to the pyjama pants' bottom hem.

Saturn screamed, "Arné!"

He had never heard his name shouted in such a manner. It made his heart stop for a second as he watched the dog shaking Saturn's leg like he wanted to rip it off. He quickly took his stick, and with one hard blow, he beat the dog on his head, making it cry as it tore a piece of cloth from Saturn pants. Arné hoped that it would have been hard enough for the dog to flee away. But it was not. It started to growl at him instead. The high pitch of a whistle in the wind made the dog turn its head. Arné looked on as Saturn crawled behind him. And just when they thought that things will get worse, the dog turned around and ran towards the sound. It was the watchman who called his dog back to see if it had found anything, and when the dog approached him, he reaped the piece of material from the dog's muzzle and looked on. The same cloth he would give to Principal Malin directly after he had found it and said: "the bitch tore this from someone out in the fields." Meanwhile, back in the field, Arné and Saturn caught their breath for a while, sitting on the ground. It was an event that will go on to change them forever: Arné's guilt, a duty-bound vow; and Saturn's fear, a terror for dogs.

"I'm sorry, Sats," uttered Arné. "I didn't mean to."

It was quite a surprise for Saturn that Arné somehow thought that it was all his fault. "Is the bite deep?" He asked and had a look at Saturn's ankle.

"It's just a scrape," Saturn said, partially to make Arné feel better, and partly to evade tears of fright.

"Let's go back," suggested Arné. "Miss Hope can make it better."

Saturn looked towards the mountain and considered abandoning the quest for a minute, but they had already come too far to give up now. And although it was a terrifying thing that had happened, the bite had not even left a trace of blood. "No," Saturn said and stood up. "We've already come this far, and look, we're almost there. Let's keep on going."

Arné hesitated. "Okay," he said. "But tell me if you want to go back."

And so, the two children proceeded. Arné in the front, cutting the grass with his stick, occasionally looking back to see if Saturn was doing fine, and Saturn aback, wondering what Arné wanted to unveil.

"How are you holding up?" Arné asked as he looked back in motion.

"A bit tired to be honest," Saturn grinned.

"We're going to be late for it if we'll continue at this pace," Arné spoke a thought out loud.

"Well, if you're in so much of a hurry, why don't you carry me then," Saturn joked.

Arné observed the mountain. And as he glanced back, he started to walk to Saturn. "Well. Come on," Arné said when he got to Saturn and turned around again.

"What?"

"Climb on. Let me carry you."

"I was making a joke."

"And it was a brilliant suggestion."

Saturn hesitated.

"Come on. We're wasting time."

"Well," Saturn said, "okay, if you want to."

Arné sighed and pressed forwards with Saturn on his back. He still felt slightly bad for what had happened and tried to make up for it.

"Thank you." Saturn kissed Arné's cheek from behind.

It is a good thing Saturn cannot see my face, Arné thought. Otherwise, Saturn would have seen him blush. "Don't mention it."

The grassland's hard floor slowly disappeared underneath Arné's feet and was replaced with a muddy splish-splash. They were in the march. And not long after that, the lake underneath the mountain was in sight.

"Look!" said Saturn.

"We're here," Arné said relieved.

"You can let go of me now."

"Just a couple more steps," Arné said taking a few paces farther, and on the lake bank, he let go.

It is a beautiful thing: how the mind can drift off into the eyes of nature. The sky was clear and still full of stars, slowly starting to fade into the day as they lose their glitter and shine in and above the lake and the mountain and the hills. The moon's reflection over the water broke just like the wavelets broke against the lake bank, and the wind whistled through the cat's tails growing in patches all over. Yet, for Arné, this didn't even come close in comparison to Saturn. It was a beautiful place where they stood, so Arné thought; merely not as much for its plain sight as it was for its representation. For it stood for the end to many things: it was here where the future of Saturn's life was first recorded; it was the end of their visible universe through their childish eyes; it was the end of many more things to come – though neither of the two children knew of the last.

"It's beautiful and calm, isn't it?" said Arné.

Saturn smiled. "Yes, yes, it is."

There was a moment of silence between them, in which they took off their shoes and put them away and walked towards the lake. The morning coldness of the lake's water washed over their feet as they remained still next to each other, gazing upon the picture painted by nature.

"So, now what?" Saturn asked calmly.

"Now we wait for it to come," Arné replied quickly, though as if he wanted the silence to remain. Yet, he spoke in riddles as it was presented in his mind; frankly, he still had to figure out how to show Saturn that which he wanted to.

"Maybe we could then talk in the meantime?" Saturn suggested and went back to sit on the bank. Arné quickly followed. "Are you cold?" he asked.

"A little," replied Saturn.

"Should I move closer?"

"You may."

Arné moved closer and put his arm around Saturn as Saturn's head dropped on his shoulder.

"This is nice," said Saturn. "I wish I could feel this free every day."

Arné sighed. He knew the feeling all too well. And although this opportunity to speak freely didn't arise every day, one would think that you had to seize it, conquer the moment, and say something. Still, it was ironic—after being told what to say and being prohibited from speaking at all, you lose your own sense of the truth of conversation. It becomes difficult: you don't know what to say or have too much to say, and you don't know where to begin. And where do you start? If neither person in the conversation knew what to say. Yet, the two children enjoyed the excellent company more than the converse. Their presence spoke more than a thousand words could ever express.

"Will you always be my friend, Arné?" Saturn suddenly asked unexpectedly.

"Always."

"Will you ever leave me?"

"I pray every day that I won't have to."

"I hope so too," Saturn said. "You're a perfect person, Arné. And I hope that I will have you in my life forever."

Arné breathed in and out. He knew the truth of the advent—the deformity of their future.

"So, what did you want to show me?" asked Saturn.

It was the question Arné had both hoped for and feared. But it was not yet time. "Look," he said.
The two children both gazed over the mountain. Their eyes fixed where the sun's first ray broke down in the morning sky.

B. HAVEN

Part 2

—————

Summer

BOOK III

A Dream Remembered

Chapter Seventeen

———

Left as Is

THE SUN CARED, AND SHOWED humanity; it was, if not the only, outside force apart from Miss Hope that did. Breaking dawn was beautiful. It painted twilight colours over the horizon and made it seem like a holy timeless existence that granted wishes – a sign of good hope, a symbol for new beginnings. And as the sun extended its mounting, it painted nature with all its divine colours: the sky, its own blue; the hills, their green; the mountain, its shades of brown; and the lake, it's vivid. Then it painted Arné and Saturn's pale faces, before – like magic, where it covers its own art – the landscape came to life. Fish started to spring in and out of the water. And a gentle breeze blew from the mountain over the lake right through the leaves of trees and cat's tails. It was keen on the children's faces, still sitting next to each other, as they cuddled up a little bit more.

"Isn't it just beautiful," said Saturn.

"Almost as beautiful as you," Arné said meaning every word he spoke. And although he had flirted with Saturn many times over with similar compliments, he didn't think that Saturn actually knew how much he meant it. He fancied Saturn, both inside and out.

Saturn bumped him against his shoulder and blushed. "Oh, shut up," Saturn grinned, "you're such a tease, you know that?"

Arné blushed, turning his face so that Saturn would not see. And for a moment longer, the two children sat firmly next to each other with similar thoughts about making this moment last forever. A dominant consideration which had crossed their minds many times over. Too many times for children their age.

"You know," Saturn said, "we'll probably get caught when we go back."

"Yeah," Arné sighed, "I know," he said deplorably.

And though it was a perilously terrible thing that may occur, their captivity sustained within the tranquillity of creation that portrayed their words and feelings.

Arné gazed at Saturn, gawking off into the dawn. "So why go back then?" he suggested.

Saturn's head lifted from Arné's shoulder in shock. "What!" Saturn said stunned and surprised.

Arné had a severe smile.

"Oh! Come on, Arné," Saturn continued, "you can't possibly be serious."

"Why not?"

"Like we have somewhere else to go."

Arné looked towards the mountain and sighed. Despondency invalidated his impression. And so, for another moment there was silence between the two children again.

"If only in a perfect world," Arné said. He stood up and walked towards a big rock partly situated in the lake. "And for that world, I shall strive," he mumbled to himself softly so that Saturn couldn't hear him.

Saturn looked towards Arné with compassion. He was busy walking around the rock, though as if he was looking for something. "What are you doing?" asked Saturn.

Arné walked a little bit more. "Voila!" he said as he took up a fishing rod from behind the rock.

Miss Hope had given Arné the fishing rod (she always gave the kids of the orphanage gadgets to amuse themselves). Her decision to provide Arné with the fishing rod had come with her discovery of Arné and Saturn's 'outings.' And though she never encouraged this sort of behaviour (for the ominous consequences), she knew that she would not be able to keep them from it. She thus felt like they needed something to occupy them when they were down by the lake.

Saturn smiled. "Fishing? Really?" Saturn said and watched Arné climbing to the top of the rock.

"Of course," Arné grinned, standing at the top, swinging the rod over his head and putting the hook in the water.

Saturn looked on, pacifying in the sun.

Arné looked over. "Want to try it?" he chirped, though as if he tried to change their moods.

"You know I don't like it," Saturn grinned from afar.

"Yeah, yeah, yeah," Arné teased. "But just for once come and try it with me. Who knows? You might turn out to like it after all."

"And what's the catch?"

"No catch," said Arné. "Well, unless you get a fish on the hook," he continued ironically.

Saturn stood up and went over to Arné. "But I don't even know how to—"

"I will show you," Arné said, reeling in the fishing line.

Arné stood behind Saturn, now holding the rod in hand.

"Like this?" asked Saturn.

"Perfect," said Arné. "Now we have to swing it over our heads," he continued, as he helped Saturn throwing the hook into the water.

"Like this?" Saturn asked again.

"Perfect," Arné repeated, "now, you just hold it. It's a game of patience." Arné let go and sat down next to Saturn with his feet in the water. It was somewhat ironic of him to have stated that. Mentioning patience. Patience was a word quickly taught yet not easily learned (assumingly for many, not only Arné). He knew the feeling all too well. As patient as he was, he was impatient and controlling.

"So, what's the thing you wanted to show me or talk to me about?" Saturn asked with the rod in hand.

"I'll show you after you catch me a fish," Arné joked.

Saturn laughed. Arné hasn't ever been able to catch a fish with only the hook; somewhat ironic for Saturn watching Arné trying to fish without bait. "And what gives—" Saturn tried to say, but the line was suddenly pulled.

Arné jumped up.

"Fish! Now what?" Saturn said.

"I don't know," Arné said panicky. "I never got this far. Pull it in."

"Help me," Saturn laughed.

The two children were joyfully startled. Grabbing on to the fishing rod-like their lives depended on it as Arné turned the pulley, reeling the fish in. Overwhelmingly they moved around in small paces until Saturn slipped and grabbed hold of Arné's arm, ultimately catching him off guard, and they both tumbled down the rock. The ring around Saturn's neck broke loose. And an unexpected dry floor stopped their fall – though as if they had disappeared.

Chapter Eighteen

Engagement

WITHIN THE CONNECTIVITY OF THEIR eyes, time – as they contemplated it respectively – had come to a standstill: fainting away into an anosmic abyss that made the coffee house perfumed, like clean air, and the customers' conversations echoing into silence. For a moment, right before their senses devised – in parts – their subjective thought over time into a perfect cohesiveness, it was though as if they had seen each other's lives from a distant past. Arné's mind riddled within the astonishment that the one thing he had once been sure of - about his existence, wherein all his joy, triumph, and his company had lain – returned from a virtual absence. An absence in which he had come to find himself again. Thus, the moment he laid his eyes on Saturn was a moment of great revelation. He knew that life, as he had come to know it, has changed yet again. For the better, he knew not. But though he had once given up – a time which brought him closer to his sense of self, a time in which he cleared his mind – the present juncture gave him a second opportunity; though as if he had never renounced it in the first place, but merely only paused. So, he was ready to engage again—a last leap of faith, rather than sound reasoning. Yet, within this balance of faith and reason, Saturn's reverence tended more the scope of purpose. The knowledge presented itself as an open book, an offer you can't decline – though as if Arné was the passport into the hidden past. Saturn's white flag waved over dependable philosophies and set a new sight on unravelling a novel assemblage of memories' recollection.

"Hello," Saturn greeted slowly with a sense of disbelieve. "Can I take your order?" Saturn asked slowly as the habit intervened the bewilderment.

"Hi," Arné said and paused for a moment. And just to make sure that his eyes weren't deceiving him, he read Saturn's name tag. Joy told him about one week ago that Saturn had left town. But this was unexpected. He didn't think that Saturn would come here. Within all the disbelief, he struggled to find a word to say. It took him a moment. "How— are— you—?"

Already their converse did not cohere. Though as if, Arné and Saturn were still trying to find each other within the abyss, they had felt a moment earlier.

"I'm well," Saturn answered, "thank you for asking." Still slowly and calmly spoken. "And yourself?" Saturn uttered after a brief pause.

"I'm good," Arné said. "Ye, ye, ye—good," he continued, though as if he needed to verify everything he stated. And without thinking twice, he spoke again. "Would you like to join me?"

At first, surprised, Saturn looked around the coffee house. "I work here," Saturn whispered with a grin. And suddenly, like a saviour, Patience, who had overheard their delicate conversation when she served a couple at a nearby table, walked up to Saturn.

"Not this afternoon, my dear." She took Saturn's apron and stood next to the table as she showed Saturn the seat. "Now, what can I get you two?"

Within all the amazement, Saturn did as Patience said and sat down.

"The usual," Arné quickly glanced towards Patience.

"One breakfast," Patience noted.

Saturn, still stunned by the occurrence, remained silent. A vague expression from Arné and an open gaze from Patience brought confusion, then realisation.

"Oh," Saturn uttered. "Breakfast, yes. Thank you, Patience."

"Two breakfasts coming right up," Patience grinned and walked away.

If a needle had fallen on the table, you would have heard it ping between Arné and Saturn. And though the silence brought back too many memories between them, uncomfortable wouldn't have been the word either of them would have used to describe it. As it was, the silence bore a type of excitement.

"Saturn," Arné finally developed the reserve. His expression intended to recognise a pleasant surprise.

Saturn interpreted the address otherwise. An assumption: a recitation of the nametag still fixed on Saturn's uniform. "Yes," Saturn said, "and you are?"

"Oh! Of course, where are my manners? I apologise," Arné said, "my name is Arné."

It sounded familiar, Saturn thought. "Nice to meet you."

"Likewise," Arné said with charm.

Patience brought their orders. "Two breakfasts and coffees," she said as she placed the dishes on the table and walked away.

Eating their meals, they continued their conversation.

"So, have you always been from around here?" asked Saturn.

"No. Actually," Arné said. "I lived here once, a long time ago, and only moved back here about a year ago." He took a sip of his coffee. "How about you?"

Saturn paused for a moment to think. "Not really. Though I did spend some time here as a child. Actually, in the orphanage house just outside of town."

"And when did you move back?"

"Last week, in fact. I needed to get away." Openly spoken, Arné's next question made way for their conversation.

"Away from what?"

And so had started communication. A converse that proceeded freely and friendly; a discussion about their lives before they had each moved back to town. Yet, Arné continued diligently and prudently over the matter. Narrowly mentioning the manor. He couldn't say too much and expose himself, and he couldn't tell too little and conclude the conversation. So, he left out the delicate details about the unorganised timeline he had come to live (he did though mention Joy and Grace and Miss Precious).

In contrast, Saturn said everything from waking up in the hospital to just before they met each other in the coffee house. Yet, Arné had good intentions and reason for withholding the information. The amusement both felt made the time fly. They had decided to have a late lunch additionally. By the time they were done, the sun was already busy setting, and they had decided to go on a walk. Arné paid the check, and they strolled to a nearby bridge over a pond.

They both stared down and regarded the koi fish swimming around with a swan in their midst. And as Saturn looked back up to view Arné, his shirt collar revealed a burned mark on his neck. And suddenly, within that moment, Saturn retrieved another memory:

It was dark out in the field, as the stars were their only guides. The house behind them as far away from them as the bright moon. It felt like relieve.

"Come on, Sats!" a boy shouted within a laugh. "We need to go."

"Arné, wait for me," Saturn laughed. "I'm coming," Saturn shouted back, running towards the boy, and taking his hand.

They laughed as they continued to run together.

"To the hills, my love! Soon we'll be free," the boy said.

It was short and potent. Enough for recognition. "Arné?" Saturn looked up bewilderedly.

Arné shifted, lifted his head.

"I knew someone who went by that name once."

"You did?" Arné said, surprised.

"Yes. Though a long time ago, I did."

They looked at each other with startling amazement.

"You were that boy, weren't you?"

Arné was speechless.

"The boy in the orphanage house." The memory made Saturn smile. "Oh! How we used to slip out of that house to go to the lake." And although Arné knew it, Saturn did not. "Arné? Don't you remember me? It's me, Saturn."
At that point, Arné was still very much confused. Surprised, but confused. He couldn't believe it. *Could it be?* he thought, *could it be that Saturn actually remembered?*

Chapter Nineteen

Signet

ARNÉ'S FAINT SMILE WAS THE realtor of a tragic revelation. An affirmation. And a glance into Saturn's eyes communicated adversity insofar that Saturn knew which enquiries were out of the question. Yet both felt dazed. For what they saw in each other was prosperity in what they had both lost and surrendered.

Visibly affected, Saturn contemplated Arné's eyes. They had come to speak more than his tongue. "I'm sorry," Saturn apologised. "I didn't mean to—I didn't—"

"That's okay," Arné intervened. His behaviour seemed slightly mysterious.

He must have had a good reason for not wanting to talk about it, or maybe it was all just happening too fast, Saturn thought. Whatever was haunting his concealment, was Saturn's liberation. And so, the evening had come to an unfinished end – even though they didn't ill-separated.

The first thing the following morning, Arné went over to the coffee house. The smell of cooking made him ache for breakfast, yet it didn't matter. He went straight over to Patience behind the till and made a hello sign at Saturn, though as if he was up to no good and smirked like a naughty kid as he did. Patience was surprised to see him this cheerful.

"Have I ever told you how much I enjoy the food here," he smirked again.

"What do you want?" sneered Patience.

"I was wondering if I may steal one of your employees for the day?"

"You were wondering if you may steal our only employee for the day," Patience joked.

Arné smiled as he looked toward Saturn, not knowing what was going on, and back towards Patience. "Please."

Patience called Saturn. "Just bring Saturn back safely."

"Always," Arné said as Saturn approached.

"You called?" said Saturn.

"It seems like Mister Arné would like to take you on a second date."

Saturn smirked as Patience beamed and walked away. "Is that so? And just where did he think he wanted to take me?"

Arné laughed. "The house. I wanted to keep it a surprise, but I thought it best if surprises are kept at a low."

Saturn undressed the apron. "That sounds nice."

Within moments they parted and set out to the manor.

It has a different feel to it, Saturn thought as they saw it from a distance. For within only a few recollected memories, Saturn could already see much adjustment. There was no grassland anymore, every seeming corner of the veld around the house had been replaced with endless rows of lavender fields. And from afar, the place looked different too; it didn't look gloomy anymore;

instead, it looked attractive in front of the mountain and the hills set in its background. Arné unlocked the lock of the old and rusty front gate. And as he pushed it open, the ring from its rusty screws grabbed onto Saturn like a beast's claws that revealed another memory:

Like the gates had come to open, the gates opened again in Saturn's mind. And though the distant memory held much vagueness within its presentation, fear excelled. Exemplifying in truth. The car was suffocating, insomuch that not even an open window would have been able to fix it. In front, the two social workers spoke pacifyingly, trying to keep the two children calm. Aback Jupiter looked brave. He knew that he had to look after Saturn from that moment forward. He was accountable, and he took ownership stoically. So, Saturn clutched onto his hand, consumed within the emotion and resulted in the two social workers' calm speech echoing into silence. The next thing Saturn remembered was the car coming to a standstill in front of a big house and the passenger door sliding open like a curtain revealing a middle-aged woman with loving brown eyes.

"Hello," she said, spoken with much kindness, almost like how an angel would sing you to sleep. "Saturn. Jupiter," she continued. "We've been expecting you. My name is Hope. Do you want to come and have a look at your new home?" Her voice allured the two children from their seats, yet never letting go of each other's hands.

"Saturn," Arné's voice rung like an alarm clock pulling Saturn back into reality. The memory faded as Saturn looked on. Arné was already standing on the other side of the opened gate. "Shall we?" he said.

Muddled, Saturn walked forwards. "Yes, sorry about that. It brings back a lot of memories."

Arné was astonished. He couldn't believe that Saturn actually started to remember. What, though, was a mystery to him. Yet he understood the feeling. Even he would still get some memories of the house now and then – not all of them the best ones. "That's okay," Arné said concerningly. "Just let me know if you want to go back."

Saturn nodded in accordance. But it would have been foolish to turn around now, for the recovery of knowledge awaited. They followed the gravel road towards the house, meeting Earnest on their way. He was busy looking after the fields as they approached him, making quick introductions and continued on the route towards the manor.

Saturn's eyes swept over the house with evaluation, comparing it to the memories. The grey brick walls appeared lighter, and the surrounding grass greener. The enclosing gardens furnished the outside with fertility, decorating it with worth. Then, Saturn's eyes caught fear. For what Saturn saw was the direct diametrical illusion of what was presented in the entourage. Saturn's eyes lifted and caught sight of a part of the manor's roof. A tower smeared with the black richness of smoke stains along the walls that enumerated: the building was once on fire. Suddenly, Saturn's eyes caught the sun's rays flashing from behind the house by looking up. Blinded. And as Saturn's eyes closed, it revealed another memory:

It was night. The house's lights already cut as it was cleared from any unwanted noises, except for two children softly gossiping.

"What are you doing up at this hour?" whispered Saturn.

"Shouldn't you be in bed?" Arné tried to change the subject.

"I was going to the bathroom."

"Then go. And then go to bed." Arné said, rather promptly and walked away.

His behaviour was out of the ordinary, Saturn thought. And it made Saturn remember the times Arné wrote in a diary, though it does not sound out of the ordinary, as it was, he was sleeping while he did it. Though as if he was sleepwalking, but just writing to himself instead. Saturn decided to follow him. Though a few paces behind so that Arné wouldn't notice. He stopped at Principal Malin's office and entered. Saturn followed and upon reaching the door, pushed it a little ajar. Principal Malin always adored Arné, for some unknown reason Saturn did not know. And remembered how he would ever let Arné get away with murder. So, it was interesting to hear what they would talk about tonight.

"Arné," Principal Malin greeted friendly.

"Hello, Sir. I was wondering if we could maybe speak?"

"Well, what seems to be the problem?"

"Well, Sir. I wouldn't really say that it is a problem. But more something I would just like to tell you. Think of it as, asking for advice and guidance."

"I'm always happy to help. So, tell me. What is it?"

Arné paused for a while though as if he was scared. "Well, Sir, it's about me, and my life really…"

"Yes," Principal Malin said concerningly. "Go on…"

"Well, ever since I was a young boy, I felt different." Arné paused. "You see, Sir, some years ago I found out that I could—well—" he struggled to find the words to say and then cut to the chase, "well—travel in time."

"Is this some sort of a joke, Arné?" Principal Malin intervened with slight anger.

It was the first time Saturn had ever heard such a tone coming from Principal Malin to Arné.

"No! Not at all, Sir. I can prove it. Miss Hope will come into your office any second now asking you about your day and why you haven't gone to bed yet."

Although surprised, Saturn got a fright. If what Arné said were true, Miss Hope could show up at any minute now. And with no delay, Saturn hid away for a moment. A moment in which, surprisingly, Miss Hope did show up, and a few seconds later walked out. When Saturn returned to the door, resting even more ajar than before, it gave Saturn a clear view into the room. Principal Malin now stood in front of Arné. He rose his hand and with one clean swipe, hit Arné across the face. A blow that made Arné fall to the ground a few feet away.

"Devil!" Principal Malin shouted. "You're going to hell, boy. Don't think my hands are cut off. I've dealt with one of *you* before."

Saturn's face turned pale. It was an alliteration alike, resembling the scare Arné will come to bear forever. And within that moment, Saturn realised why Arné behaved as he did earlier on. It was because he was afraid. Afraid that his trust and love for Principal Malin could betray him at any second soon. As it did.

The vibrating and ringing in Saturn's pocket served as a pullback into reality. Arné watched as Saturn pulled out the phone and answered.

"Hello."

…

"Hi. Yes, I'm fine. And yourself?"

…

"No. Please don't come."

…

"Because I'm figuring things out for myself."

…

"I will be sure to do that. Umm, listen, can I call you back? I'm a bit busy at the moment."

…

"Okay. Love you too. Bye." Saturn ended the call and put it back.

"Who was that?" asked Arné.

"My brother. He's a bit worried about me."

"Sounds like a good guy."

"He is. I suppose. Just a bit overly protective, I guess sometimes."

Arné laughed. "Come on. Let's go in, and I could fix us something to eat and drink," he said and led Saturn to the kitchen.

Saturn looked around. It was much homier than Saturn could remember. Although some final additions were still to be made, it felt like everything was already in place. After lunch, Arné showed Saturn around the house and had a friendly conversation until night fell upon them. Saturn decided to sleep over, and Arné prepared the guest bedroom.

Heinrich Dittrich

Chapter Twenty

———

Fraternal

JOY HAD A SECRET OF his own. Something he had never told anybody, not even Grace. He had always managed to ground himself within all the chaos surrounding the lives around himself, though as if he was glue; time never allowed him to subdue. His mother's adverse habit of bringing bad guys home after a few too many alcoholic beverages, Grace's drug addiction, and Arné's timeline mess-up were only some of the glares. Yet, he had endured it all and managed to become a doctor (with a particular goal to study his 'condition'). This, too, was the reason why he had never told anybody about his own little confidence. He could travel in time, a condition that inspired him to become a doctor. Though he hadn't used his gift much, for he soon discerned that what he had was not a gift. Not at all. Never. It was something else. Something darker. And it had made him come to hate time as a whole. Mostly the inevitable past. For as he had come to realise, you can't change certain things: you can't go back to change the past, and you can't go to the future to change it as well.

He felt powerless in this regard every time he saw Grace going into the rehabilitation centre. It was a place he had come to hate as much as time, for it too reminded him off all the things set out of his control. As it was, Grace was in and out of rehab for the past year, unable to keep a steady job, nor let go of the drugs. Something that had occurred a long time ago. Something Joy had hoped to put behind them. It broke his heart, seeing Grace that way. But he remained faithful to the person he loved and promised to help. He met Grace in high school. And though they were cardinal directions apart outside, in class, they were best friends, that is, until Grace started to date another boy from school, something and somebody Joy did not endorse ("he was a bad guy, you could see it from a mile away"); it was one of the reasons why their friendship broke.

After that, they did not speak. Then, one day – peculiarly – Arné introduced them to each other (without his knowledge of their pre-connaissance). As it was (though it is not the purpose of this novel to elaborate on these relations, it is required to be told), Grace had therapy with Miss Precious, and she and Arné had met each other through this mutuality. They became very close friends too, so close that Arné had shared many of his secrets with her. Though she had not come to bother herself with them or be included in them as much as Joy was; she had problems of her own.

Joy still remembered his first initial thought when he found Grace in the hospital after her breakup with the same guy he warned her about, *why would a girl that beautiful try to kill herself?*

The entire night was still clear to him, though as if it happened yesterday.

"You can't save people like that, they have to save themselves, but you can help. You can be there your attitude towards her will change not everything, but a lot. So can you teach her to love herself too," he remembered Arné saying to him in the hospital, right before he felt inspired to approach Grace again. Arné had heard himself of Grace's accident, that was why he was there. And one might call it luck, but for them it was destiny.

"You shouldn't hang out with fuckers like that," Joy told Grace.

"So, who should I hang out with? Basterds like you?"

Joy smiled. "That was insensitive. You know I'm."

Grace looked at Arné for guidance. Arné winked. Though as if he said, "take that leap with him. He's a good guy. Don't you worry about that."

Since that day, their friendship started to blossom again, until it grew into a relationship. Their love story actually started after Joy learned of Grace's breakup with the guy; yet, too soon realising that the guy had left Grace shattered, empty, and a patrimony drug addiction. Grace never spoke much of her family, and Joy had never met them.

The rehabilitation centre was still as Joy walked around the gardens to look for Grace.

"Joy!" he suddenly heard Grace shouting.

She ran up to him, and the moment she reached him, she jumped into his arms. "Oh! How I've missed you," she said.

"Not as much as I've missed you!" *She looks good*, Joy thought. She was herself again, that same free-spirited person he had come to know. Her hair, blond hair – almost golden – shone again and the dark rings surrounding her beautiful blue eyes were gone.

"Shall we go?" Grace asked and kissed him. "I'm already packed." Grace was in a hurry to get out.

"Let me just sign you out, and then we can be on our merry way."

The nurse at the desk was kind. Though she was a serious person, she always tried to cheer Joy up whenever he visited.

"She's one of the good ones," the nurse said. "Problems. No. Confused. Yes. Like us all. But she's a keeper too. Keep her safe."

"I will," Joy greeted and walked towards Grace, waiting in the lobby.

The sun outside felt like pure freedom. The fresh air within the wind pushed forwards like an aspiration towards a better life. Grace had missed these feelings. Not that she wasn't allowed outside when in rehab, but it was the mixed feeling of freshness and freedom that she had longed for.

"I can't wait to get home," Grace said.

Joy smiled. "I was actually thinking of talking to you about that."

Grace's spontaneous personality made the conversation easy. "Oh. Yeah. Go on."

"I was actually thinking about not going home."

"Where do you want to go?"

"I was thinking about Arné's place." He had decided that it might be a promising idea. Better in fact than the city, just to get away for a while. It might do Grace some good, he thought. So, he had already taken leave from his work and told himself that for at least the next year, he'll spend some time with Grace and Arné.

Grace paused for a while. Thinking. Not about going, but about Arné per se. More specifically, a particular thought between them. For Grace witheld a secret from Joy too; only because it wasn't her place to disclose it – that was Arné's place. So, it made her think about the revelation again upon hearing his name, though only the brief, preliminary discussion:

"Oh my! Arné," Grace said, "I don't believe it. You're his b—" she couldn't finish, partly because Arné interrupted, partially because she was rendered speechless. "You're going to tell him. You have to tell him!"

"I will," Arné said sadly, "I will think about it."

"Well, if you won't, I will," Grace said seriously.

This was in fact the other reason why their relationship had once ended all those years ago: Grace had this secret of Arné she couldn't keep from Joy. Though she never told him—instead, she ended her friendhip with Joy.

Grace pulled herself back to reality with the fear of suspicion. "I would love that," Grace said. "I miss him. How's he holding up?"

Joy knew what Grace was talking about; Arné's fate was clear to them both. "Strongly," he answered and continued, "and I have to add, and all I'll say is yesterday when I spoke to him, he told me that he met Saturn again."

"In that old town?"

"Yeah."

"Oh," Grace said. "Then what are we waiting for. We need to go and pack."

"Already did," said Joy.

They both climbed into Joy's car, and they made way to Arné's.

Chapter Twenty-One

_____

Balance

T HAT NIGHT WAS LIKE A mirror: it showed a deep reflection, and in that reflection, Saturn stood at a fork in the road. To the left was the way much taken: as it was, Saturn could succumb to doubt in which Arné's life had lain in mystery and distrust—judgement without thought. To the right was the road less travelled: philosophy—thought before judgement. Saturn lay in bed in the manor's guest bedroom, staring deep into that reflection and choosing to take the latter. Though it was the most enigmatic, it was also the one that struck Saturn as the most prominent in knowledge and prosperous in life. It was in a sense more congenial: though Saturn's own life was a mystery too, their lives showed an inexplicable sign of connectedness, though as if Arné's life holds the key to unlocking the secrets of Saturn's own. Yet, a feeling of fear had come to hover over Saturn in a haunting spirit; that there lies something deeper, something darker, something intractable.

The following morning, by the break of dawn, Saturn got on the phone to talk to Patience right away, cancelling another day of work. Surprisingly and strangely, Patience sounded glad to hear Saturn staying at Arné's and doing things with him. Nonetheless, right after the phone call, Saturn entered the kitchen, finding Arné preparing breakfast for them.

There was only one thing on Saturn's mind. Noting else. Not even a hello, how did you sleep? "We need to talk," said Saturn.

The strict tone in Saturn's voice had Arné concerned. "Yes, of course. What do you want to talk about?" These kinds of conversations typically only result in one thing, leaving.

Saturn quickly glanced out of the kitchen window that overlooked the mountain where the lake was. "Not here," Saturn said gravely, "there," looking back towards the mountainside and with no delay, walked out the back door.

Arné threw cloths over the food he was busy preparing and followed. It was a quiet road. Arné walked behind Saturn for the entire way until he found Saturn by the lake looking at the mountain.

"Is everything alright?" he asked concerningly.

"This is the place we normally came to when we had enough of the orphanage house. It was the place where we could be who we wanted to be. We were free here. We weren't afraid to speak our truth here," Saturn said, still looking at the mountain.

"You remember?"

"I do." Saturn remained still for a couple of seconds. "Now I want you to tell me. Tell me the same thing you said to me on the very first day we had met." Still looking at the mountain.

Arné went to stand beside Saturn. "I can travel in time," he said, though as if he regretted his own life. He knew that if Saturn's memories returned, these kinds of subjects would arise.

"That explains the event at the Botanical Garden then?"

"Yes."

"And have you lived all of this before? Am I merely a do-over of some other time?"

"No," Arné said. And turned to face Saturn. "Never. Once I have lived a day in my life, I can't live it again."

"I see," Saturn said. Yet within the sense provided, it all still seemed disconnected, though as if nothing made sense at all. "And you have travelled before?"

"I have," Arné's tone turned to regret and misfortune.

"How much?" Saturn asked curiously.

Arné remained silent.

"If you can't answer that," Saturn said, Arné response suggested a lot, "then tell me how many days, do you have to live?"

Arné turned to face the mountain again. And with all the regret and misfortune that had ever come his way, he pronounced his sentence within one single breath that shook his entire body. "Just a little over a year."

It shocked Saturn as much as it shook Arné, turning to him though as if a doctor had just announced that he had only one year left to live; and so, it was that that sentence had changed everything. Though there were so many more questions Saturn needed to ask, it seemed insignificant through Arné's eyes. Saturn empathized: Arné had only one year left to live, and Saturn wasn't going to make it more difficult on him; certainly not by compelling him to tell his entire life's story in that regard.

Instead, Saturn thought, *allow the memories to come back in time, and take it from there*. Speechless, Saturn turned facing the mountain again.

"What's on your mind?" Arné asked.

"I don't know." *A lot*, Saturn thought, with an over-occupied mind.

"Come," Arné said calmly. "We can talk some more later." He looked towards the house as a car approached it from afar, leaving a dust trail behind it. "There are some people I would like for you to meet."

Grace and Joy were already busy unloading the car when Arné and Saturn showed up. And the minute Grace lay her eyes on Arné, she ran towards him shouting his name.

"Oh!" she said, kissing him on his cheek. "How much I have missed you."

"Missed you too, Grace," said Arné.

"Arné, buddy," Joy said, placing a bag he had just unloaded on the ground. "Long time no see, uh." Arné laughed as the two friends greeted each other.

"It's about time you guys came to visit." He then turned to Saturn. "Joy, Grace," he said. "I would like you guys to meet Saturn."

Grace was the first to greet Saturn, and just after that, Joy stepped afront to meet Saturn.

"Hey, haven't we met before," he said, though he knew all too well who Saturn was, he had only met Saturn once in his life before. "That's right. In the botanical garden," Joy said pensively.

"That's right," Saturn grinned back quickly, trying to hide what had happened that night. "I tripped and fell when you came to help me up." Saturn tried to shift the subject into another direction, denying the truth. Yet it was bizarre how Joy didn't suggest the two strange men. Though as if they weren't there. Though as if they did not exist.

Joy nodded, and Grace took over the conversation as usual. "Well, that was just the longest ride ever," she joked.

"Road trip," Joy said sarcastically which made everybody laugh.

Arné and Saturn helped to carry all the luggage into the house.

"To the guest room?" Joy asked Arné as they walked in front.

"Uhm," Arné hesitated for a second. "Actually, Saturn stayed in there last night." He paused for a moment; he didn't know why he said that. There was more than one guest bedroom. "But there's another one, don't worry," he added.

"Oh," Grace uttered. "So, you'll be joining us."

"Oh no," Saturn said quickly. "I'm actually staying in town. Last night was an exception."

"No," Grace said. "You must stay. Please stay. I feel like we can connect," the spontaneous, free spirit spoke in Grace. "I won't take no for an answer."

Saturn glanced towards Arné and smiled. "Oh, I don't know. I don't want to intrude."

"No, you won't," Grace said. "See, I'll ask Arné for you. Arné, can Saturn stay with us? Please."

Saturn laughed.

"Well," Arné said, "we could go and get your stuff later on today if you like."

Saturn grinned as Grace gave the answer. "So, it's settled then. You'll stay. Joy and I can catch up on some sleep while you and Arné can go and get all your stuff."

So, how quickly the decision was made, had it come to pass. As Joy and Grace caught up on some sleep, Arné and Saturn went into town to fetch all of Saturn's things.

The bell tolled as Arné and Saturn entered the coffee house, and their appearance dragged Patience to the door to meet them each with a hug.

"Look at you two," she said, "I know it's only been a day, but it feels like a week." She had grown quite fond of Saturn already. "How are you two doing?"

"Good," Arne and Saturn said.

"What can I get you two?"

"Actually," Saturn said. "I— We wanted to talk to you."

Patience smiled by the way Saturn spoke. It indicated honesty and congeniality. "Yes?"

"I know you and Faith have done so much for me. And gave me a job…"

"Oh, Honey, it was the least we could do."

Saturn didn't know how to go about it and decided to say it, as difficult as it seemed. "I must thank you a lot. But I recently decided to move in with Arné and would like to know if it's okay if I stop working here?"

"Oh, Honey. You don't have to ask. Of course, it's okay. It's your life, after all."

Saturn and Arné proceeded to pack everything upstairs (not that there were a lot, and it gave Arné the impression of the time they were still living in the orphanage with little if no belongings). As they came downstairs, Faith and Patience waited for them to walk them out. They both didn't seem to care that Arné and Saturn had only met two days ago. On the contrary, they seemed to embrace and endorse the event. Arné and Faith stood by the entrance and looked at Patience and Saturn loading Saturn's things.

"Have you thought about what you'll do once Saturn remembers?"

Arné kept quiet for a while. He has thought about it, yet he had no answer.

Faith looked sad and severe. "If there's one thing I've learned, Arné, in my life after I've met Patience, it is to be there. Just be there for Saturn. Without judgement.

Arné nodded and thanked Faith for everything he, too, has done.

Saturn settled into the guest bedroom after getting all the things from the Coffee House's upper apartment. Joy and Grace had taken another prepared bedroom in the house. It was dark by the time everybody was settled in. While Joy and Grace still caught up on some sleep, Arné and Saturn had prepared dinner. After their dinner, Grace and Saturn preceded the men to the sitting room, exchanging their life stories as Joy and Arné cleared the table and did the dishes.

"So, how's she holding up?" Arné asked Joy concerningly.

This was the first time since Grace was admitted into rehab that Joy and Arné had spoken.

"Honestly, right now she's more concerned about you, but otherwise, I don't know. I guess all you could do is wait and see."

"Don't worry," Arné said, "she's a strong person. She'll get through it."

"I hope so. I really do. But I think it'll do Grace good to stay here for a while. I think it will do us both some good."

"I think so too," Arné said. "Have faith, Joy."

With the table cleared, the dishes washed, it was hardly any truth that everybody was tired after the day's events. Joy and Grace went to their bedroom, and Saturn and Arné to their rooms, respectively.

Chapter Twenty-Two

———

Power

DREAMS STARTED TO APPEAR AS nightmares, and they followed their appropriate memory, waking up on the hour to some distant memories of how the house had haunted Saturn.

There was the nightmare of solitary:

Miss Hope trembled up the stairs with a faint cold breath breathing on her shoulder. It was night – a perfect time, for hardly any of the staff was awake at this hour.

Saturn was just about to fall asleep when the dorm's main entrance suddenly jolted open; startling every child awake therein. "Miss Hope?" Saturn said sleepily as Miss Hope laid a child down on one of the beds. Saturn's heart pounded with fear.

"Saturn," Miss Hope said. "You have some water?"

"What's wrong, Miss Hope?" one of the other children wanted to know. They looked up and saw a petite figure lying on the bed, though as if in a dying state.

Saturn rushed over with a water bottle and handed it over. "How long has he been in there?" Saturn referred to solitary. As it was, the basement of the house was the station where misconduct was dealt with. And though never admitted into that dreadful place, Saturn could only have imagined what horrors must have had taken place in there. Every time examining the children's faces that showcased it all; the children's visages always appeared in a vegetated state after the staff had discharged them.

"Two days," Miss Hope said, giving the water to the child, rather shyly, though as if she didn't want to admit the truth to the children. The fact that they would sometimes have served their sentence for, as much as, days on end. Though depending on the severity of their misconduct.

"Two days!" Saturn said. "What for?"

The answer, Miss Hope didn't have, and she continued with an entirely different question. "Where's Poppy?"

"She was found outside of bed wanting to go to the restroom," one of the other children said.

This was, in fact, the reason why Saturn and all the other children feared solitary a lot. For it wasn't much the cruelty of solitary itself that had struck fear in their bodies as much as it was wherefore they had been sent there. For sometimes, even the mildness of things – like asking for more food or being caught out of bed after curfew if you wanted to go to the restroom – would have bought you a direct ticket into solitary for a night.

There was the nightmare of child labour:

Proper education was hardly the case at the orphanage house, though cultivating the infertile land was. The

192

children developed the area surrounding the orphanage house day in and night out, though they never got to plant any seeds. And the land would ultimately have turned back into a weed forest. Thus, restarting the cycle again. It is something to keep the children busy with, as the staff would always say. Still, the team called it scholarship – making up educational fantasies – whenever a visitor (to whom the children weren't allowed to speak, or were too afraid to talk to) had arrived.

There was the nightmare of vulgarity:

"Worthless piece of shit," a staff member had once told Saturn, making way for himself as he jolted Saturn against a hall's wall on his hurry way. "Am I glad my child would never have to marry you?"

Though children were not allowed to speak such language, it didn't stop the personnel from cursing the children. They were often called worthless: nobody wanted them – or ever will – and they were a complete and utter waste of space. The incidents were strikes through the soul. Nothing could compare to it. Nothing could prepare you for remembering the teachings that the personnel were right, the children wrong, and Principal Malin a god.

And then had come the nightmare of silence which had endured in age:

Saturn didn't manage to fall asleep again for the rest of the night after that. But if anything, those memories motivated Saturn to stay with Arné. Though the hardships they had endured solely and togetherly induced a potent idea, they needed to rest together. And not leave each other willingly, like they had been forced in the past. It had come with a strange sense that Arné was going to do the same.

Laying in silence on the edge of the bed, Saturn watched the sunrise through the window. It was a smooth finish to the nightmares—something demonstrating more hope. And as much horror it had borne all throughout the night, the blithesome laughter coming from Joy and Grace's room turned the house untroubled.

"Hi," Saturn suddenly heard, and turning around and seeing Arné with a mug of coffee in his hand. It painted Saturn's thoughts full of joy.

"Hi, come in," Saturn grinned.

"I would have made you some," Arné lifted the mug, "but I didn't know whether you were awake or not."

He entered the room as Saturn smiled. "So, you rather came to stalk me instead?" Saturn joked.

"Well…" Arné didn't know how to respond. "If you put it like that – now I feel bad."

"I'm joking," Saturn grinned.

Arné laughed. "I would offer you mine—"

"Well, it depends on how full it is," Saturn interrupted. "Let me see." Saturn took the mug from Arné's hand and took a sip. "Thank you, you can go and make yourself some now," Saturn joked.

Arné laughed and went to sit on the lower side of the bed. "How did you sleep?"

Saturn turned a bit more serious. "I…" Saturn hesitated. "I'm still getting used to it."

Arné nodded. "Well, if there's anything I can do to make it better, just ask."

"I will," Saturn interrupted.

"Well then, I'll leave you to yourself for now. I'm making breakfast if you want any. It'll be ready in about thirty."

"I'll be there," Saturn said and, as soon as Arné went out, got ready.

It smelled of bacon, egg and toast as Saturn entered the kitchen. Joy and Grace came running in and out, grabbed a few bites, eager to amuse themselves outside in the lavender fields, and went to the lake. Arné and Saturn's conversation went from the orphanage house's gloomy subjects, and everything Saturn had to remember, to the merrier topics of what Arné had done to the place. And it was not until Arné drew warm water into the kitchen sink after a couple of hours when Saturn suddenly turned silent.

"What's wrong?"

Saturn looked out of the window. Joy and Grace's positive behaviour, as Saturn revered, was provocative. *It is beautiful: they were still so young and had so much life in front of them*, Saturn thought and turned to Arné. "I just can't believe it. It feels unfair. I just got my friend back, and now he'll be taken away from me again." Arné closed the tap and sighed speechlessly. "I'm sorry. I shouldn't have brought it up."

"No. That's okay," Arné said and placed some dishes into the sink. "If you had one year left to live, how would you do it?" he didn't mean for advice.

"If I had one year left to live with someone, how would I live it?" Saturn rephrased the question. "I don't know. I wouldn't want it to stop. Not ever."

"And what if I could make it appear longer," Arné said seductively.

"What do you mean?"

"I mean, what if we could live it again after it is done. I know that it is not forever. But it will certainly feel longer."

It was an idea that would shape their future and change the rest of their lives forever. Saturn glanced out of the window again. "Like an illusion?"

"But it would be real," Arné added, troubled by the idea. A thought that could not leave his mind.

"I have to admit, it sounds promising. I wouldn't want it any other way," Saturn said. "But is that even possible? How would it work?" Saturn added concerningly. "One year that appeared as two?"

Arné looked deeply into Saturn's eyes. "I mean," he said, "what if we live every other split second of this year, beginning to end, and then come back to live it again." Arné paused. "Like a memory."

"Like a dream," Saturn proclaimed at the same time.

Chapter Twenty-Three

———

Order

IT WAS ALREADY TOO LATE; by the time Joy and Grace had entered the living room, Arné and Saturn had already made up their minds. Outside it was getting close to dusk, inside it was way past dawn. And by the seriousness portrayed through both Arné and Saturn's visages, Joy and Grace were halted by their entrance. The room appeared in a mess, and it will come to be the witness for Joy's last conviction. The coffee table stood fast, swept clean from any prior items which had filled it before Arné and Saturn had tackled it. They packed the area around the table as they were replaced with a large calendar that occupied the whole of the coffee table. The chaos drew a straight line towards the messed-up bookshelf from which the diary was taken with a few books lying on the ground. The calendar was scribbled on with a red marker pen, though as if it was analysed thoroughly.

"Hey, you guys," Grace said hesitantly. "You alright?"

"What's going on here?" Joy asked concerningly.

They walked up to Arné and Saturn who looked like timid children who had done something wrong.

It took them a moment to proceed, but finally succeeded. "Well—Saturn and I—" Arné struggled, "you know how I can travel in time."

Joy looked concerned. Already by the sound of Arné's voice, he could tell something drastic had been considered.

"Well—Saturn and I, we have this idea." Arné glanced at Saturn.

"Yeah," Grace said.

"Well—" Saturn intervened.

Their hesitance didn't make Joy, nor Grace, feel comfortable and what they were about to proclaim wasn't thoroughly thought through.

"Well, we were just talking about how we just ended up meeting each other again," Saturn said, "and how it's all unfair that we'll be separated again soon. Well—we thought of something that might give us a bit more time."

"Go on," Joy said like a strict parent.

"So, we thought about travelling in time in a way that we will only live every other split second, and then at the end, we can come back and live it again. Though as if we will live the following year twice," Arné continued.

Why not just live it once the first time around all of it, was Grace's initial thought, but ultimately decided not to mention it. On the contrary, Joy's reaction was critical when they told them all about their plan. And the first word which had come out of his mouth was: "No!" He looked towards Grace and then back towards Arné and Saturn as they went to sit on another sofa in front of them. "Have you gone mad?" he uttered. "Can't you just for once in your life choose to live the normal chronological life?"

And indeed, it was a good question that provoked Arné's thoughts. As it was, this was what he was customed to. He didn't see life in any other way than a mere representation of an unorganised timely fashion. Time-travelling has and always will be who he is. Yet, it didn't change his mind. Nor was it convincing enough for Saturn.

"Do you know what this can do?" He paused. "To you? To Saturn?" He barely gave Arné and Saturn chance to defend their side of the argument. "The complexities. The complications."

Suddenly Saturn took hold of Joy's arm. "Joy. I know that you are concerned about us. But this is our decision. Our lives." Saturn tried to calm Joy down a bit. He looked like he was going to lose it. Worried as well. "But I do not understand what you mean." Saturn continued. "Explain it to us," calmly said.

Joy proceeded without allowing for any interruption. "You know the butterfly effect," he said. "You see, Arné has the gift to travel in time, but only in his life span. You can't go back one hundred years nor to the future one hundred years unless you were still alive at that particular point in time, and what makes it even more complicated, is that you can't live a single day twice. Now, with that being said, if you were to go to the future and find the lotto numbers, for example, and come back and then win the lotto that specific day in the future would have changed. Now, for the catch, because you would have already lived that day in the future and so will not be able to live it again, and you will only remember the day you had lived and not the "now" actual day of that specific timeline. Now, I won't argue that in small quantities this seems relatively harmless. But in more substantial amounts… This could bear some grave consequences."

"Yet, I don't understand what you mean, Joy, how does this apply to what we want to do?" asked Saturn.

"I'm trying to say and explain to you—that you can't know for certain what the outcome of all of this might be. Something that looks like something small and innocent and harmless can turn into something bigger, unexpected chaos. Moreover, you do not know for certain what your experiences will be like the second time around. Nor even how the other will react to it or even what they shall relive."

"Is this even possible? I always thought that you can't take someone else with you," Grace, who sat as a spectator, interjected pensively, "so is it possible allowing for another person to travel in time with you?"

"Yes," Arné replied quickly. "I had done it before."

Joy looked confused. He did not know that this was possible, and he had never tried it himself before. Though he would never. Arné's life portrayed enough of a warning sign for him to never divulge such a thing. He wouldn't be able to live with himself if something ought to go wrong. Yet he looked towards Arné and Saturn and Grace, worried, but with accordance. "Have you thought about when you want to do it? Or start?"

"Tonight," Arné and Saturn said together.

Chapter Twenty-Four

———

Left up to

THE HOUSE HAD ALWAYS COME to find a way to haunt them. Even in the future. Though still unknown that this blessing in disguise would also become their refuge, it would come to pass in the most peculiar of paces. As it was, Arné and Saturn, two beautiful candles lit by hope; and like candles above water, so were their fall towards the dry floor of the orphanage house about fifteen years into the future. Though as if life, before the water could quench their fire, had found a way to bring them back together. Yet, it was safe to say that it had come to Saturn as the biggest of surprises, although Saturn, at that time, would not have called it that.

As it was, the first thing Saturn could remember was being disoriented and confused. "Arné!" Saturn called. "What just happened?"

"This is what I wanted to show you," Arné said.

Saturn felt off balance and couldn't find a foot to stand on, and the mixed sensation of light-headedness and dizziness didn't help much. *That doesn't make any sense*, Saturn thought, *I can't see anything*. Although too quickly thought, Saturn's sight started to reappear gradually.

The room was unlit, and though it was night and dark inside too, Saturn could make out a fireplace, some bookshelves, sofas and armrest chairs, a coffee table and in the close distance, another figure.

"Where are we?" Saturn said. "My neckless. It's gone."

Saturn and Arné got back their senses and the first thing Saturn saw, was a young, middle-aged man standing with them in the room. The room had a strange sense of familiarity, though as if they had already been there before, maybe even lived there previously; still, it appeared altered. The man in the room stared right at Saturn. And like the room he, too, was familiar with his brown hair and tanned skin. Yet Saturn was afraid. Mostly uncertain.

"Who are you?" With a pounding heart, Saturn shouted, grabbing the closest thing that could have been used as a weapon for protection. A candle opera. "Don't come any nearer!" Saturn said.

"Sats," Arné finally spoke. It calmed Saturn down, for it made Saturn feel accompanied. "Can't you tell? It's me, Arné. Put down the candle opera," Arné said. And lo and behold it was Arné in the body of a thirty-year-old man.

What, Saturn thought. "What," Saturn said. Turning around and reflecting in distant mirror, Saturn saw a person all grown up and moved when Saturn moved. "Is that... But how... Arné! What's happening?" Saturn lost control of the untenable situation. "My ring is gone."

"We travelled in time," Arné said calmly, walking evenly towards Saturn. "I'm sure your ring is back in the past and fell off as we travelled."

It had not come as much as a surprise that this was possible, as Saturn had overheard Arné once telling Principal Malin about it, yet it felt unreal. Though as if it was a dream to which Saturn will wake up from at any given moment. Saturn was not the only one who had questions. Arné too had some of his own. They were back at the orphanage house, and it arose much curiosity. It took Saturn some time to adjust to the thought about what had just happened. A time in which Arné had made them each a cup of tea to repose and have a relaxing conversation before it got more serious. So, they went to sit on one of the sofas in the sitting room where they had appeared a moment earlier.

"Why did you bring me here?" Saturn asked.

"Are you angry?"

"No, I wouldn't say that."

"But…"

Saturn remained silent for a while and sighed. "I do not know." Saturn stood up and walked toward a big window that looked out onto the mountain and the hills. "Why did you bring me here?" Saturn said again, full of confusion.

"I wanted to show you," Arné said and walked towards Saturn.

"Show me what?"

"Hope," answered Arné.

And though in a strange sense it was hope. Saturn felt free. Nobody was here to threaten them, though as if they had escaped it all. "Is that lavender fields?" Saturn looked curious.

"It looks like it," Arné said. "Let's go and have a look, shall we?"

Arné and Saturn went outside to have a look. The emotion got the better of the two, and though it was dark, they started to run around in the fields like two children would. They must have not noticed how far they had run, and the next moment they stumbled over a rock by the lake.

"Look," Saturn laughed. "Isn't it beautiful?"

"Almost as beautiful as you," Arné said as they sat firmly next to each other and enjoyed the view of the landscape.

The moon hovering above the mountain by the lake made them happy, like a balloon in a child's hand.

"Can we stay?" Saturn asked out of the blue.

Arné sighed in dismay. "Saturn," he started, "I wish we could. I really do. But you see if we would come to live this life now, we will at the end have to go back and live our lives at the orphanage. As we can't live a single day twice, yet you need to live all."

Saturn looked sad.

"Come on," Arné said and took Saturn to the big rock he used to stand on and fish. He then took another sharp rock, and together they engraved their initials on the bigger stone.

"Does this make it ours?" Saturn asked.

"This makes for us a beacon," Arné said. "Somewhere, we belong."

Then for another while, Arné and Saturn sat next to the lake. They glared at the moon and the mountain and the hills like they did back when they were little.

"Shall we go?" Arné said softly.

Saturn nodded and breathed hard. Then they took each other's hands, and before they knew it, felt the cold wetness of water covering their bodies.

Part 3

Autumn

BOOK IV

———

A Dream Dreamt

POV Arné exc. 25 & 32

Chapter Twenty-Five

———

Left Direction

IT WAS LIKE A CERTAIN type of gravity that pulled them towards the house, even, from outside its borders. Arné and Saturn could not escape it. And though it would be a lie to say that the thought about running away had never crossed their minds, both Arné and Saturn felt each their own sense of moral obligation, towards Miss Hope and the other children at the orphanage house, to stay and fight through it.

Saturn and Arné stood up from the shallow water in which they had fallen only a moment earlier. A gentle breeze wavered over their shivering wet bodies, as the warm sun had entirely replaced the moon in the clear blue sky, giving them a warm embrace.

"I'm soaked!" Saturn said and started to laugh.

Arné laughed too. He felt exhilarated. Though as if a significant burden was lifted from his shoulders, though he knew the worst was still to come.

"Me too," he said, giving Saturn a helping hand from the lake.

"Wow!" Saturn said when they got to the dry land and fell into a sitting position like they had run a marathon.

Arné went to sit next to Saturn. "It's something, isn't it?"

"It sure is," Saturn said and looked towards Arné. "Promise me that we shall do so again some other time."

"I promise," Arné grinned.

Tranquillity swept over their souls for yet another moment. Their attention shifted to that of the mountain and the hills behind it, seeking out the freedom they had come to feel. However, within the contemplation of the landscape, Saturn felt like something was missing. Like they forgot about something. And with a deep breath and a single touch on Saturn's neck, it then suddenly hit Saturn hard in the gut.

"My ring," Saturn said. "It's still missing."

*

A turn was on the way. Miss Hope could feel it; the butterflies in her stomach were not there for the excitement. It appeared like fate through her eyes as she ran up and down the orphanage house, searching for Arné and Saturn. *Where are you two*, she thought, and for a moment blamed herself; she was the one who so too often would encourage them liberally. Yet, never had they remained gone for so long. She was afraid and out of breath; her beating heart confessed it. The principal was not in a great mood that day, and she didn't know whether or not she'll be able to talk them out of the strain and trouble. Miss Hope jolted into at least ten different children, all hastening down towards the cafeteria. They couldn't be late for the most important meal of the day.

"Dear," she would say, "have you seen Arné and Saturn by any chance?"

And the answer would always remain the same. "No," the children would say, "sorry, Miss Hope. I have not."

My goodness, Miss Hope thought, *what have you two done?* She carried on the search.

"Miss Hope," she suddenly heard. The voice approached her from behind and sounded turbulent.

Miss Hope turned around. "Yes, Malin," she said, "Is everything alright? Can I do something for you?" She pretended as if everything on her side was clean and without worry.

He looked irate, and two strange men both dressed in black stood next to him like bodyguards. On the contrary, their facial expressions appeared composed, though as if they didn't have a care in the world. "Do you know by any chance where Arné might be?" Principal Malin asked, and by the sound of his voice, it didn't make the answer any more comfortable to give.

"No," Miss Hope said, composing herself. *God forbid what he'll do to him,* Miss Hope thought. "I have not seen him this morning."

"Well then," Principal Malin said, looking at the men next to him, who strangely appeared stiller and more silent than turtles. "I'm sure he'll be in his room then. Probably still sleeping or doing something he shouldn't do. This way, boys," he said and headed straight towards Arné's dormitory.

"Yes, maybe," Miss Hope suddenly said, stepping in their way. "Let me go and check for you."

"No need, Miss Hope. I'll go and get him myself."

Miss Hope was running out of options. She needed to buy the children some time. "Malin," Miss Hope uttered swiftly. "I just remembered two children passing me who said Arné was already downstairs at the cafeteria. I'm sure he'll be down there by now. All the children have already gone down. I'm sure he's among them somewhere." Though she knew this was unfortunately not the case; Principal Malin and the two strange men went ahead to the cafeteria themselves. She knew that the cafeteria would also be so densely packed with the children that one would hardly make out between all of them where a single child was sitting. Miss Hope might have just saved Arné and Saturn's lives, although it didn't stop her from continuing the search.

*

Arné leapt back into the lake the minute he heard Saturn's cry. "It must be here somewhere," he said as he splashed through the water in search of the ring on the surface.

Saturn followed. "Oh, no!" Saturn cried. "I can't have lost it!"

"Don't worry. We'll find it."

They were at it for a couple of minutes when at last Saturn kicked back with the thought that they can't stay there forever and search since they need to get back to the orphanage house. "It's no use. We'll never find it now."

"Let's keep on looking," said Arné.

Saturn sighed and exited the lake without any words.

"I'm sorry, Sats," Arné said as he walked towards Saturn. "It's all my fault. I didn't mean for this to happen."

"That's okay," Saturn said regretfully, "I know it's not your fault."

"I'll get you a new one. Or – I will come back to look for it again tomorrow," Arné said, trying to cheer Saturn up.

If only you had known what sentiment that ring bore, Saturn though and smiled faintly.

Chapter Twenty-Six

———

Decisions

NIGHT FELL FROM A RISING star at dusk. It was time. I reached out my hand with a particular type of delegacy that in an identical touch in which I could see Saturn blush while taking it, made both our hearts flutter. As it was, our hands had not come to know this type of intimacy since the day we had met again a few nights ago.

Before, though, I had taken hold of Saturn's hands, Joy, Grace, Saturn, and I had dinner. Grace's keenness made her suggest that Joy and Saturn should prepare the starters, pudding, and salad, while she and I should prepare the main dish. In fact, it was the first time ever, Joy and I had not seen eye-to-eye (not on this level, though); Grace recognised this. Joy was mad at me and unable to get all crazy at Saturn; that, and she must have thought that Saturn could maybe get through to him. We hopped around the kitchen in awkward silence. Grace tried to be the antidote as she would try to break the reserve.

"So, what are you guys making?" she would ask Joy and Saturn quirkily.

Joy's responses were always as abrupt as his emotions. "Chilli cheese toast, salad, and mousse cake."

Saturn must have felt too awkward to say anything at all.

And with no other return question from Joy, Grace tried to fill up the silence again. "Well, Arné and I are making creamy chicken and mushroom pie," she said and rejoiced, "Joy's favourite." She gave Joy a kiss (he couldn't say no) and continued.

Around the dining table, the stubborn awkwardness prevailed. The tension and concern which hovered over the house hadn't made it the most exquisite dinners we've ever had, and we sat around the dining table that evening, though still enjoying each other's company, in a way. Yet the most spoken phrases being: "could you pass me that," or "can you help me with this."

That was, apart from Grace's interferences. You could tell she didn't like the censorship at all. "I love what you've done to the place," Grace said, trying to break through both the taciturnity and communication. "What do you think, Joy?"

"Thanks," I said.

"Looks good," Joy said.

Saturn looked on.

"Well, I just love it. I'm so proud of you," Grace said, remained silent for a while and then continued again. "So, what have you guys planned for the rest of the year?"

"Mostly just staying here," I said.

Saturn nodded.

"What do you think they can do, Joy?" asked Grace.

"Sounds good," he answered.

And like this, the dinner continued until Joy was the first to break the silence after Grace.

"I'm done," Joy said. "I'll start washing up." He left the table and went straight to the kitchen.

The spray of running water tapping into the sink coming from the kitchen rouse me to my feet. I followed Joy soon after he left, not finishing my own dessert. "Excuse me," I said and walked to the kitchen.

Inside the kitchen, I looked at Joy, thinking I had to do something. I understood that he had every right to be concerned as he was, as he was the one who frequently helped me every time Saturn had disappeared, back when I was still in a search.

"Joy," I said sympathetically as I approached him standing in front of the sink.

"Are you sure you want to do – go through with this?" he asked as he placed some dishes into the sink and turned around to face me.

I placed my hand on his shoulder. "Yes," I said. *I'm keeping a promise*, I thought. "I wouldn't do anything I'm not certain of doing."

He breathed in and turned around again. He must have known that he couldn't change our minds. "Then I'll support it," he said. "If that's what you want to do."

So, after dinner, with Saturn's hands in mine, I ushered our way. And as I did, I recited that poem within the glint of moonlight shining in through every windowpane. That same poem that I had described so many times over before. The poem that bounded us to a destiny of fortitude through which our hearts may find a place we knew and where we belonged.

> "Let's set forth to the great green hills, my love.
> Let's set forth whence the mountain greets the sky
> And cries the lake beneath dawn's lonely eye.

Let's set forth thence to be for our behove."

Then we sat, and Saturn's blue eyes sparkled within the reflection of flames coming from the fireplace. Alas! My displacement came to a sudden end; the alienation in which my being was put, settled. The unfulfillment of my entire instinctive life lifted from my soul—all to a point where I couldn't care much for the initial purpose of my existence.

Joy and Grace were bystanders, and as they looked on, watching how Saturn and I sat facing each other with our knees crossed in the twilight zone in front of the fireplace, Grace was calmly holding Joy's hand on her lap. As it was, he was still very much concerned.

"Are you ready?" I asked.

"I am," Saturn grinned.

Saturn's hands shook in mine, and frankly, I think half of it was coming from me. Yet I held on to them with a subtle touch through which I said, *I'll never let go,* though I knew there will come a day when I must.

"Close your eyes," I said.

Saturn's eyes closed with a soft smile. I did the same. And as I did, trying to focus on our peculiar travel, I spoke that rhyme which gave us hope and courage all those years ago again. For all, focus, inspiration, and rendering Saturn a type of familiarity and calmness.

> "Let's set forth to the great green hills, my love.
> Let's set forth whence the mountain greets the sky
> And cries the lake beneath dawn's lonely eye.
> Let's set forth thence to be for our behove."

And so, the metaphysical realm in which our lives were turned, amended.

Chapter Twenty-Seven

———

Consequences

I OPENED MY EYES TO a sight so familiar, that in its significance, it felt like a ring on my finger: I didn't feel any difference and change, yet I knew it was there. The circumstance had me both frightened and pacified at the same time, yet it was visionary. There was a future. And although it seemed so far off into the shadows, it appeared with clarity full of hope and sense. So, I was ultimately forced to smile because of it.

"Can you feel it?" I grinned.

"Yes," Saturn grinned back. "Yes, I can."

"Open your eyes."

And suddenly within that motion, when I saw those blue eyes again, I felt a blow to my chest and arms surrounding me. The abrupt moment caught me off guard, and it left me off balance. Saturn and I had fallen to the ground. And for a moment as we lay still on the floor, and listened and felt each other's heartbeats, an evident embrace had reshaped our touch. And within the resistance of its termination, I felt that I had finally fulfilled my sense of affinity for place and situation in the fullness of time itself.

Meanwhile, in the background, Joy and Grace's anticipation grew more potent by the second.

"Do you think it actually worked?" Grace whispered to Joy.

"I don't know," he answered with deep concentration and pensiveness. "They look the same to me."

"Well, I don't think that it'll actually change them physically."

"I don't know," Joy said, again absorbed by the moment.

Their suspenseful breathing with us in the room shifted our attention. Saturn looked up towards me and sat up straight. "I'm sorry."

"No," I grinned, "Don't apologise. I liked it."

Saturn grinned back.

"So, how does it feel?" I asked out of curiosity.

"Almost like gravity," Saturn answered with a face that showed a subtle hint of excitement and amazement. "Though as if you can't feel it, but you know it's there. Yet strangely, I can see it, and I can hear it."

It was an accurate definition, evinced in expression and behaviour, of our cognisance that in this anomalous situation, even by our own standards, we were incipiently living every other split-second together. It was stimulating.

The night had come to an end with our affirmation towards Joy and Grace who had been waiting in great anticipation to hear the words coming from our own mouths, that we were, in fact, living every other split-second.

"So…" Grace had whispered to us. It made both Saturn and I smile. "Did it work?" Joy only sat and regarded.

Saturn and I stood up, and like two newlyweds, we held each other's hands and smiled and blushed at each other's presence, and we walked over to where Joy and Grace were sitting on one of the sofas.

"It worked," I said with relief, even if I had to admit it myself.

And in that instance, I had said it, I could see the tension relieved from Joy's body, yet I saw an undertone of caution.

On the other hand, Grace displayed much more excitement, throwing her arms around us, and then quickly retaking Joy's hand. "So now what?" she asked with joyful tears in her eyes.

Her question made me realise that I, myself, had not yet thought thoroughly about the ordinary things we will be occupying ourselves with, although we knew we would stay here. But Saturn's agile approach to answering that question had me stunned. "I guess we keep going on. Living each day, day by day, though as if they were our last."

The account of the following two days was simple enough. On the first we hadn't done much except for enjoying each other's company and getting used to the idea that we were, as it was, skipping to live every other split second in our lives. Though I must say, the peak of the day had come when we had a surprise visit from Earnest, Verity and their baby, Alina. An occurrence had turned into a sociable lunch, where we discussed the renovation plan for the house. Though we weren't in much of a hurry.

As it was, our relationship was friendly, yet it stayed within the boundaries of professionalism. And though we did see of each other often out in the fields, visits were episodic. It goes without saying that they had their own social group, and if they weren't hanging out with them, Alina still took up the majority of their time.

That evening we went to the beach to have a BBQ. As I recall it, it was Joy's idea.

"We haven't celebrated yet. And this certainly calls for a celebration," Grace thought, "What shall we do?"

"Yes," Joy and I agreed to do something. I was glad to see that we were still able to see eye to eye on some things.

"Something together…" Saturn said pensively.

Grace turned to Joy. "I don't know," he said. "Maybe we could go to the beach and make a bonfire. And as we haven't had dinner yet, maybe we could have a BBQ as the night is still young enough," he suggested, and it suited us all.

The day after that day, by the looks of it, Saturn had settled in more comfortably. That is why, when, after we had breakfast, we enjoyed a cup of coffee out on the porch, and I, myself a cigarette, Saturn had brought up our discussion of the house once more.

"So, you were saying the other day that you were busy renovating the house," it sounded though as if Saturn wanted an input. It made me smile.

"Yeah," I said. "Still some work to do though."

Saturn grinned. I knew some other squeaking door passed Saturn's thought. Yet, Saturn remained still, though as if Saturn did not want to come across as being invasive and intrusive to offer some input.

"You know you could help, though. I mean technically this place is yours as much as it is mine now," I spoke out of love. Disregarding any form of legal documentation.

Saturn grinned. "I'd love that."

We went into town soon after that to do some grocery shopping, did some window shopping, and looked for things to either help us or add to the house's renovation.

It was out of the blue that we had found ourselves passing Faith and Patience's café. We went in. Had a quick talk over lunch about how things were going and went our separate ways again.

That evening after dinner, Saturn and I went to the library.

"You haven't read to me ever since I can remember," Saturn said, dragging a hand along the books as the other was leading me.

I said nothing and smiled. The library had me thoughtful; to think, somewhere among these books was the one which had brought me this far. The one that told me how much time I had yet to live. Moreover, Saturn's words had me curious about how much Saturn had remembered about our past, as this was undoubtedly one of those memories.

"I want you to read to me," Saturn said seductively.

"I don't know," I said. I wasn't the best at it; Saturn knew that. Still, when we were even younger, Saturn always got me to do it. "You know how bad I am at it."

"I don't care," Saturn said, "read me something," and turned facing the books in search of one.

"Which one?" I asked too soon as Saturn pulled one out.

"This one."

"Which one?" It was a collection of five novellas.

And as Saturn pointed at the title, my eyes raised. "You remember?" I said. The story's name was *The Dreamers*, and I used to read it oh so many times to Saturn when we were young.

Saturn did not reply to my original question. "Read to me."

We sat in one of the window seats, having made ourselves comfortable with a blanket and cushions. Saturn's head resting on my shoulder as I turned to the first chapter of the novella:

I.

T HE DAY HAD PRESENTED FIVE gifts. The first gift was given, after a black Cadillac escalade – number plate "Harrison" – had appeared out of a forest and pulled over in front of a Victorian styled Manor-house, as the passenger door slid open revealing its precious cargo. With the scent of saltwater nearby, a gentle breeze blew through the brown hair of the little girl climbing out.

Silently, she stood to the front double door of the house. And as they opened, the second gift was presented, revealing a middle-aged lady with wavy brown hair that accompanied her red dress. She reached out her hand towards the girl. And with a subtle movement with a grin across her face, the girl took it. "Hello," she said, "you must be the one she's been waiting for."

The house was warm on the inside. Though as if it was called home. And as the lady ushered the little girl through the hallways of the house, it appeared more so.

Finally, they stopped. The room was much different from all the others inside the house. It appeared in a twilight-like atmosphere because of the lit fireplace. Two chairs in front of the fireplace matched a coffee table between them, and a grand piano on the far-right-hand side of the room precipitated sociability.

The girl's glance towards the chair next to her had presented the third gift: a senior lady with locks of grey hair and blue eyes. The girl sat comfortably, though as if she knew the lady.

"I have a dream," the girl said emotionally.

The lady sat in silence as she turned her attention from the fire to the girl. "Do go on, my dear, dear young child," she said peacefully.

"Everybody told me that it's impossible. That I should not even bother and just give up."

The lady took the girl's hand and looked into her light brown eyes. "Oh! My dear child, sometimes you should learn not to listen to what other people have to say. And only follow your heart." She stood up, letting go of the girl's hand and walking over to another part of the room, which appeared to be a kitchen. "Would you like some tea Miss Harrison. It seems that we have a long talk ahead of ourselves. And tea. Well – tea has its way of easing all of it."

The little girl smiled at the way the lady spoke. She nodded politely in the affirmative and watched how the lady got their tea ready.

"Oh my," the lady startled as the kettle blew. It made the little girl smile. "It seems that our tea's ready." She took everything and placed it on the coffee table with some honey and milk. "Now, while we wait for it to cool down, let me show you something," the lady said and took the girl to the grand piano.

The little girl's eyes grew big. "Wow, it's beautiful," she said as she explored the keyboard around.

"My dear, would you come here quickly," the lady called the girl to the keyboard as she pulled the piano's chair from it, creating a space for them to stand. "Would you like to know what I desire most in life?" she asked.

"Yes, I do," the girl said. "Please do tell."

The lady remained still for a while and smiled. "It's to play this note, right over here. One tone higher than the last." She referred to the void space with no note after the last note on the right-hand side.

"But isn't that a bit impossible," the girl looked confused and touched the empty space. Then looked back to the lady.

"Yes. Precisely, my dear," the lady said seriously. "We all want something dear to our hearts. Sometimes appearing as an illusion that we can't ever have it…"

The lady stood still for a moment in anticipation of a positive atmosphere and continued with wisdom words. "But if you concentrate and work very, very hard, and listen with an intended ear, and imagine yourself into a space no-one has ever come to enter before, you might just hear a ping."

The girl looked intrigued by what the lady had said. And glancing at the empty space again. "What will you call this note then?" the girl asked.

The lady grinned, and as she spoke, she enlightened the room with both a sense of knowledge and light, knowing well that it would have been a 'D' on the keyboard. "The Dreamer's Note," she said. And that was the fourth gift the day had presented.

I closed the book, having realised that Saturn had fallen asleep. So, I carried Saturn to the guest bedroom.

Chapter Twenty-Eight

———

A Plan Set

IT WAS THE THIRD DAY, and so far things had turned out better than I had expected. Saturn and I were getting along very well, and – if not the most essential element – Saturn looked happy. Things were slowly starting to fall into place, and though we haven't had much time yet to continue the renovations, getting our lives sorted was, at first, the priority. That morning while I was preparing breakfast, Saturn entered the kitchen, looking concerned.

"Hi," Saturn greeted just as I broke an egg into a pan. "That smells nice. What are you making?"

"Hi," I greeted back. "Usual," I grinned. "Did you sleep well?"

"Better, thanks."

The silence solicited development. "Something on your mind?"

"I was wondering if my brother might come over and visit. Well, him and his family."

Of course, I said yes. I must lie if I should say that, at first, I didn't have my own doubts about it. I wanted Saturn's brother to come and visit, but how much of everything which had happened, I did not know Saturn was willing to tell – or even how much I was ready to speak.

Nevertheless, Saturn hopped onto the phone ecstatically to invite Jupiter and his family for a visit. I overheard part of their conversation.

"I was wondering if you and Serenity wanted to come and visit maybe?"

…

"There is actually someone I would like you to meet."

…

"I think so."

…

"Okay! I'll see you soon then. I'll text you the details."

…

"I love you too."

…

"Bye!"

And so, at the appointed time the following weekend, Jupiter, Serenity, with Happiness in her arm, showed up at our doorstep. We made quick introductions and had them settled in at no time. The weekend flew by like sand through an hourglass. It was congenial and sociable. We had occupied ourselves with either something in town or by going to the beach. If we weren't doing that, we made some small talk about the house (both negative and positive).

"I can't believe I'm back here again," Jupiter had said at a time.

"It is a bit weird, isn't it," I had answered.

"Though I must say that I love what you have done to the place," he said and turned to Saturn. "I can see why you love the place."

However, it was fortunate – even if I should say it myself that it was a depressing thing to admit – that the conversation about the actual reasons behind Saturn and my motives for staying at the house was not brought up. But that thought came all too soon. As it was, it happened the evening before they left. As I recall, it was in fact, I who had slipped my tongue within a conversation about the renovations of the house.

"And to think we'll have to start all over again after this year has ended," I said jokingly. I didn't think what I was saying. And the smile on my face left me as soon as it had come.

Saturn made me a face.

"I don't understand," Serenity said.

A million thoughts had crossed my mind. One of which was, *how do I tell you this?* I've always found it awkward telling people about my ability. The reason for this was apparent to me. And yet till this day, every time I had to, that one memory in particular always sprung up: the time I told Principal Malin.

"Well, I actually wanted to tell you guys…" Saturn began and continued explaining what we were busy doing. Jupiter took it more natural than Serenity. As it was, she had more trouble wrapping her head around the subject.

Joy and Grace quickly after that left the table feeling, what I thought they felt, somewhat awkward around a silent table where nobody wanted to touch their food. Serenity and Saturn cleared the table as Jupiter and I went to the living room.

"Listen, Arné," he said earnestly, "What do you expect from all of this? You know how it all will end. You will have to leave Saturn behind in the end. Have you thought about that? Saturn has a good heart. And I can only see one outcome to all this… It isn't a good one."

He was protective, I understood that, and only wanted to look after Saturn. Nevertheless, it left me speechless.

"Why not just leave Saturn out of it all?"

It was at that moment he spoke when Saturn entered the room. "Leaving who out of what?" Saturn said jokingly. Jupiter turned to investigate the fire. "Arné," Saturn turned to me. "Could you please go and check if Serenity is okay. I need a quick word with my brother."

I nodded and left, and never heard the conversation they had. And the following morning when Jupiter and Serenity left, neither of us spoke of it.

The weeks that followed that weekend were calm and still. Joy and Grace had left for his mother's, as he had announced one day before they had left: "We have thought about leaving for my mother's for a little bit." And of course, I endorsed it, not only for the sake of their wellness, but it would also give Saturn and me some time to spend together alone. However, the glance Grace had given me just after Joy had mentioned his mother, made Saturn suspicious in the eyes that there too was unfinished business, yet nothing had come from it – at least not for now. As for Saturn and myself, we spent those weeks either occupied by going into town, going to the beach, renovating the house with Earnest's help, and working in the fields with him too.

Our relationship was growing stronger with each and every one of those passing days of the weeks. But it was not until one day, when we had found ourselves in the lavender fields, occupied by a conversation in which I had apologised for my behaviour that evening in the botanical garden more than a year ago (leaving out the particularities), that it was set in stone. As it was, it happened in the most peculiar of ways.

"Do you hear that," Saturn said and looked around.

"Hear what?"

"Shh," Saturn placed a finger on my lips. Then, I heard it too. Something like an animal whining. "I think it's this way."

I followed as we traced the sound. And lo and behold there it was with golden fur in direct contrast to the purple of the lavender: a golden retriever puppy. Saturn got a fright, though my first thoughts were: "How on earth?" And then I couldn't help but notice Saturn's fear of the dog, as little as it was. I went over to pick it up. "Is everything okay?" I asked Saturn.

"Yeah. Fine." It wasn't, I could see that. "We should take it in. It looks like it's going to rain." Saturn must have remembered. How much, though, I was uncertain about.

When we reached the house, it was already pouring down. The puppy, which I had sheltered underneath my shirt, remained dry, whereas Saturn and I were soaked. We went in and dried ourselves by the fireplace, conspiring over the puppy. We made it some porridge and let it eat as we rested in front of the fire.

"You were so gentile today," Saturn said tenderly.

The moment, captured by the once deepest desires of my life, lived on. I revered. Seduced by the face within the twilight shadow created by the fire. A shining which I could only have painted into three words that entered my mind. "I love you."

Saturn leaned forward as I spoke, "I love you too." And blushed with a smile painted across that face. Within a slow motion towards each other, that once glorifying embrace which I had felt the moment we had started our year together, glowed into an eminent fix of some more vital connectedness as our lips met for one tender kiss.

Chapter Twenty-Nine

―――

The State of Muddle

WITH UNAWARENESS OF WHAT THE day had in store for us; the following day proceeded like the days of the weeks that had preceded it. At dawn, whoever woke up first would have made coffee and would have carried it to the other's bedroom, where we'd then sit and wake up together (though this morning we shared another good morning kiss). We'd talk of various subjects and decide on our agenda for the day. Afterwards, we'd get ready and start whatever we'd decided on after breakfast. Today, our schedule was in part, ascribed to us as we had a new member of our family. We called him Sneaky, for he had snuck up on us and in turn seemed to do it all the time as he accompanied us in the house. I went into town to get him some supplies, and while I was there, put up some posters and gave out some flyers just in case he had belonged to someone.

I pulled over in front of the café. I was thirsty and thought it well to support the local business Faith and Patience owned.

"Oh! What a surprise. Again." Patience announced when the bell tolled as I entered, and as always, both Faith and Patience were surprised to see me. "How are you?"

We exchanged pleasantries, and I brought them up to date with the latest news (that was worth sharing) in Saturn and my lives.

"Oh! I'm so happy you two met again after all that time. It just brings joy to my heart," Patience said.

I smiled, not knowing what else to do. It felt like I spoke to my grandmother. "Thank you," was all I could say until my hand, holding the posters, started to sweat just before I wanted to leave. "Oh!" I said, "before I forget. Would it maybe be okay if I put a poster up in the shop? Perhaps by the window. Just in case Sneaky belongs to anybody."

"Of course, honey," Patience said as she helped me put it up.

I greeted and just as I was about to leave, Faith came out of the kitchen and decided to walk me to my car. He has changed a lot since the day I first met him. He was kinder. More passionate. It must have been Patience. Still, though, he was scared.

"How much had Saturn already remembered?" he asked me on our way. I started to fear that he still struggled to get over his past. Afraid that Saturn will recognise him.

"Honestly, Faith. I do not know," I said, "Though I do know every day presents something new. I can see that. But what? I do not know."

Faith nodded shamefully. *Saturn will forgive you,* I thought, and I wanted to say it, but I didn't. For I wasn't sure if it was his own past vices that startled him so. He had aided in committing a crime many years back. He was never a murderer. I knew that too. Yet, he wasn't going to let it happen even if it meant surpassing his own moral values.

That evening, while I was preparing dinner, Saturn explored the house. It wasn't long after, and far from the kitchen, I heard a sheet being pulled from an object.

"Everything good?" I asked from the kitchen.

"Yeah!" Saturn said back. "Everything is okay!"

Then, I heard the high pitching tones of notes producing a melody in a warmup way. I haven't heard Saturn play the piano in what seems like forever, and it charmed me from the kitchen. Leaning against a wall next to Saturn, Saturn started to play a beautiful piece of music that filled the entire house's rooms with harmony. This was what I heard:

RELATVM VIII

a g# minor - V4

Bach's empathize
The PRAELUDIUM

Theudric-H.
W.W.W. 1

D.S. al Coda

"Your turn," Saturn grinned, turned to me and lifted the pedal and notes stopping the sound.

"Oh! Really." I laughed. "You know I can't."

"That doesn't mean you can't learn," Saturn grinned. "Come on, I'll show you."

I went over and sat next to Saturn on the chair.

"You see, it's easy. All you have to do is play one key after the other."

I tried it.

"See! You're playing."

It's not the same, I thought and blushed for how amateurish Saturn made me feel. "How does it feel?"

"What?"

"When you don't just do this."

Saturn stood up and went to sit behind me. Though uncomfortable, I didn't mind. And from behind, Saturn's hands moved over towards the keys. "Put your hands on mine and relax. No, like this."

I did as Saturn asked. Then, an intimate harmony from our hands' slow movement, hand-in-hand, created a melody in which I had fallen like a dream.

"How does it feel?" Saturn asked.

I smiled. "You're amazing, you know that?"

The melody stopped with a kiss. "Marry me?" Saturn asked.

There was silence. I nodded. "Yes."

A sudden shut of doors startled us and brought us back to reality. "Arné! Saturn!" It was Grace shouting. Saturn and I ran to the front door of the house.

Grace was holding Joy in her arms. Blood, dripping from his nose, soaking his clothes in red and his right eyebrow was bruised above his already swelling midnight blue eye.

"What happened?" I rushed to help Grace, carrying him to the living room. Joy's ankle appeared to be sprained as well.

"I'll grab the first aid kit," Saturn said.

"Two men," Joy said out of breath.

And the moment he had spoken those words, I got a fright of a familiar sight. Though too shocked to carry on with the subject I took the first aid kid from Saturn. The shock of seeing him at first glance made his injuries appear more severe than they really were, and the moment he caught his breath, being a doctor, guided me to help fix himself up.

"Did they follow you here?" Saturn asked concerningly which, for a moment, made me question what Saturn had learned; nevertheless, I did not bother.

"No," Grace said, "We lost them in town. Not that they tried to follow us here."

"Just punks." Joy added.

Chapter Thirty

The Beginning of Change

I F I COULD HAVE HAD it my own way, I wouldn't have Saturn remember them at all; as it was, I haven't thought this much of those two strange men in years. And yet, there and now, it made me wonder; I could see it in Saturn's eyes in the wake of each and every passing day just how much Saturn had remembered about our pasts. And though they were real to me too, only in the back of my mind, Saturn reacted upon their existence though as if they were imminent. Nevertheless, I tried to convince myself of other things.

The following morning, Joy was doing much better. His injuries looked less severe as they weren't too dangerous, and it made me think of what fight he must have put up if there were two of them and only one of him. It was also the same morning they heard the news. Saturn and I were engaged now. They couldn't have shown more pride. That, and we had a new member of our family; Sneaky.

And so, the month which followed that day was one of the highlights of our year.

Ambient music at dawn in front of the clear blue lake commenced the establishment of our alliance.

"Are you ready?" Joy asked as we rested a few feet away and our eyes facing away from the wedding scene, awaiting Saturn.

I nodded excitedly.

"Nervous much?" he asked.

"Just a bit."

"Everything will be okay," he said as Grace ran up to us.

"Okay," she said. "Saturn's here." She signalled for the DJ to begin the song.

Then, I turned. Contemplating how Saturn turned as well. We started to walk towards each other. Joy giving me away, and Jupiter for Saturn. My heart played an opposite beat of both the music and our pace. Before we said our vows, we looked at our company. It was a small intimate ceremony for which Faith and Patience had prepared the meals, and Joy and Grace were in charge of the venue.

Earnest, Verity, Alina, Serenity, and Happiness were there, alongside Sneaky who was never claimed. In my eyes, an ironic case that, in our individual lives, under the circumstances, an orphan puppy had found his way to an orphanage, housed by two orphans. Yet I longed for those two souls who had helped bring us together. Miss Hope and Miss Precious. Though I knew they would have been proud of us.

I turned to face Saturn and there at dusk we commenced our faithful final vow to have and to hold from that day forward, for better, for worse, for richer, for poorer, in sickness and in health, to love and to cherish, till death do us part, according to God's holy ordinance; and to that we pledged our faith.

We stayed at the house after that for the honeymoon. Joy and Grace have gone to his mother's again for a week to give Saturn and me some private space.

That evening I took Saturn's hand, and I lead our way to the lakeside. There, we sat and reflected as we glanced at the sun setting at nightfall. This was the place it started, the place where we had first truly connected. It only made sense that it would then also become the place where our old journey ended, and our new life began.

After the sun had set on our old-time together, I took Saturn back and poured us a bubble bath. We undressed each other that night, only looking at each other's eyes. It was our consent. Our souls already connecting within the passion of our hearts. And as we sat there, in the bath, teasing each other, our eyes did not lose their contact. Then, I took Saturn's hand. We climbed from the tub and dressed each other in bathrobes.

Saturn went to stand outside on our bedroom's balcony as I switched off the lights and lit a few candles. It was an unforgettable sight—Saturn in front of the stars and the moon shining bright. Bright as our loved appeared. Brilliant as it felt. It was though, as if I was in a dream, both literally and figuratively. A dream we dreamt together. I desire I once had as a small boy, wishing for nothing but this. All of this. As I stood there still and in silence, contemplating the beautiful picture, I dropped my robe. My bare feet carried me gently towards Saturn.

The skin of another had never felt so soft, and the pulse in Saturn's neck was ever so gentle: both, soft and gentle as my love. My one hand moved down and up again over Saturn's body above the robe, the other arm tenderly resting around Saturn's neck.

"Do you love me?" I whispered in Saturn's ear.

Everything that followed appeared in one gentle, quick dance: "Make me yours," Saturn moaned as the robe fell to the ground and our lips connecting after our eyes.

And so that first evening, within the fluttering of our hearts like when we had met before. Within the delicate intimacy like when we first touched each other. Within the fullness of our first embrace that reshaped our touch. Within the first "I love you" that pathed the way to that glow that connected our lips—we started to make love.

It started with our eyes. A connection that was already enough as I stood bare in front of Saturn lying on the bed. A bond that already felt physical even without any physical touch, though it did turn to that soon after. Our palms linked our bodies with a certain type of delicacy that made my heart rate rise by the second as I moved closer to Saturn. And within the heat of our combined bodies starting to rub passionately against each other, I couldn't remember the last time I had felt this loved—this secure—all which were locked by the taste of Saturn's sweet kisses. Kisses that breathed out moans that seemed like a lullaby to my ears. Breaths that pulled me deeper into a trance fixed by the passionate scent of Saturn's physique. Our love continued in an equilibrium state where the one did not overthrow the other—both of us, submissively and dominantly. It was a sensation my heart would never come to forget. And ever since then, we made love every night in our new shared bedroom.

When Joy and Grace returned after that week, things went back to normal for the most part. And the weeks and months which had passed them, whenever they were at the house, would have helped us with the renovations, something I didn't mind, or they would have occupied themselves with whatsoever they felt like doing. Every day held its own significance, like those which preceded them. Either by celebration, renovation, or amusement, or both.

Until, though, a day came after those months that was not as congenial, nor populated as those times preceding it. A phone call that Saturn had one night was the inception of the unsatisfactory situation. I remembered Saturn answering the phone, and by the first second, I could tell that something was wrong.

"We'll be right there," Saturn concluded the phone call and turned to me directly. "We need to go. That was Patience. Faith just had a heart attack."

We rushed. And by the time we pulled over at Faith and Patience's house, an ambulance was already parked out front, and the EMT's were already taking him away. As we had found out, the neighbours had called 911 after they heard Patience's cry. Faith had passed on.

Saturn spent some part of the week with Patience, giving a helping hand with whatever was necessary. Saturday, after we had learned of his death, we were all standing under black umbrellas dressed in black ties and clothes in the rain which fell like the lowering of his coffin.

The evening of the burial, Saturn helped Patience pack as she had decided to move away. We never heard from Patience again after that day. She only told us that she was staying with some distant relative and that we should not worry too much about her, for she was doing fine. And still, I heard her last words just before she left: "I have to go now dearies, you two keep now save."

His death was, in a way, the crevice into the unseen sight—enlightenment. I had seen in Patience's eyes, even just a glimpse, of what awaited Saturn and it made me think of something I had once long ago locked up and concealed very far away, a once known secret that I had chosen to forget. My journal. And I had thought as well of the future and the legacy I'll leave behind. That in a way, I'll never go.

Joy and Grace had taken up the coffee house. And it occupied them in the wellness of both congeniality and welfare. And for the months which had followed, Saturn and I continued with the legacy of the house.

Chapter Thirty-One

Change

TIME HAD NEVER BEEN KIND to me, so why should it have shown me kindness now? I lay in bed with Saturn by my side, and I couldn't believe how fast time had flown by. We were married for a couple of months now, and for me, it still felt unrealistic. Though as if I never believed that it would actually come to pass. And as I lay still, two things came to cross my mind. The first thing was the time. As it was, my end drew nearer. We had lived so thoroughly and so happily that I had almost forgotten about it. But it was so close that trying to ignore it couldn't shelter it from me anymore. The second thing was more of a gut feeling. Though as if I could tell that something wasn't right. And whether it had affected Saturn or not, I knew not.

I got up. Saturn was still fast asleep, and I decided to check on how Joy and Grace were doing. It was unusual. The house appeared in a strange sullen silence. *Odd*, I thought. Joy and Grace were usually the first ones up, bringing a type of music which filled the house up with them. I approached their room.

"Joy, Grace," I called as I stood behind the closed door. I knocked. Nobody answered. I pushed the door open slowly just in case they were sleeping and didn't hear me. "Joy, Grace," I called over with yet again no answer. I decided to go back to bed and convinced myself that Saturn and I were sleeping in and that Joy and Grace were out on an early morning hike. I thought about calling them. Just to make sure.

My phone was on my nightstand, and as I took it, glancing over at Saturn as I did, carefully trying not to make a harsh sound, I dialled Joy's number. It rang.

"Hey, buddy," Joy answered the phone. He sounded occupied. "I was just about to call you. How are you doing?"

"Good, good," I answered back. "Where are you two?"

"Oh, man, I'm so sorry. Actually, Grace and I are still at my mother's place. My car broke down I don't think that we'll—"

I ended the call with a sudden blow to my head. Timorously stunned. The next thing I knew was receiving a text message from Joy, and I immediately texted back. My mind was running wild.

Hi! Everything okay???
Joy

All good. Bad signal. :(sorry call you back in a bit.
Arné

I felt like I've been drinking all night long and now have to deal with the consequential hangover the following morning. With disbelief, I put the phone back on the nightstand with my hands to my face, almost pulling my hair out one by one. And then it struck me, with every last bit of horrid surprise left in the situation. The date on my cover screen. As it now appeared, I had woken up one month after the last night I went to bed.

My startling movements had woken Saturn up. "Hi, you up already?" Saturn yawned and smiled, but Saturn immediately turned pale and concerned by the expression portrayed on my face. "What's wrong?"

And then I proceeded to tell Saturn everything which had just come to pass. After our brief conversation in which we could firmly establish that Saturn too had, in fact, travelled with me to this date (ultimately skipping the last month).

"Well, let's just go back then," Saturn keenly suggested.

But I tried. And nothing had come from it. My ignorant choices of the past came back to haunt me all over again. I must have already lived that month somewhere else before. And all together must have faded away into the immense abyss without being noted in my journal.

Seeing how I freaked (for I felt responsible), Saturn tried to stay calm. "That's okay," Saturn said, trying to calm me down too. "We still have time."

I remained silent and shook my head. "This is the day," I said softly, but the hoarseness in my voice had made unclear what I tried to say.

"Don't we—" cried Saturn.

"This is the last one," I repeated slightly louder with the same hoarseness in my voice.

Saturn remained silent for a moment. "No," Saturn said. "No, my love. I shall meet you again very soon. Yet to live another year. By the great green hills. Here where the mountain greets the sky and cries the lake beneath dawn's lonely eye. For our behove."

And indeed, I saw the truth in which Saturn had spoken those words. That this was not, in fact, our last day together. It was, as it is, inception. And so, soon after our day was spent in its halfness (full of all its delights and pleasures), the first time I died consciously ensued:

By the mist of dusk, we proceeded to the lake. And there we waited. We held each other tightly in our arms as the moon's reflection started to drift upon the wavelets crashing on the side. Saturn must have felt my heart beat fast. For within the moment, Saturn took my face and looked me deep in the eye.

"See," Saturn said calmingly. "We are here, by the great green hills, my love. We are here, where the mountain greets the sky and cries the lake beneath night's lonely eye. We have found our behove."

I nodded my head. "I will wait for you, my love, for I know now that my high search is finally over," I said.

And so, because we still lived every other split second, I had experienced every other split second of this ending. And then I felt a strange numbness throughout my entire body, and I could feel how each individual piece of clothing I wore on that day left me too. And it was, though as if I saw the light go from my own two very eyes as it happened. And I reflected—a final thought. I'd come to wonder if I'd succeeded in the initial intention of my survival.

Chapter Thirty-Two

―――――

Left Side

THE ROAD BACK TO THE orphanage house was silent. Arné and Saturn followed their trail back through the meadow, the grassland, and the field in a great hurry. They couldn't be late for breakfast. Though they both knew they were. Within half an hour, they reached the house in all its glory. And like they had sneaked out, they snuck back in. Stop and go's all the way through the doors and corridors. Arné held Saturn's hand.

"This way," he'd say, "Stop. Okay, now we can go," he'd continue.

The silence within the house spoke. It felt, for some unknown reason, strange. It wasn't the silence they were used to. It felt different. Though like the silence before the blast. They had preceded in that fashion until a familiar voice caught them.

"Where have you two been," Miss Hope said.

Startled at first, but upon the recognition of her face, they were relieved. She stopped them in one hallway and made sure that no one else was around to see them.

"It's all my fault," Arné uttered abruptly next to Saturn who was standing with big eyes, staring at Miss Hope like they were in big trouble. "Saturn had nothing to do with it."

"They were searching for you two." Miss Hope went down on one knee and patted their shoulders, though as if she tried to clean the dust off them. "How on earth am I supposed to get you two out of this mess now?" Their wet clothes told her they were in fact by the lake. "How am I going to explain this?"

"It really is all my fault," Arné said again.

"Let's get you two downstairs immediately," Miss Hope said in rush and fear, forgetting altogether about their wet clothes. "Before the Headmaster finds you here and not there."

But she spoke too soon. "Miss Hope," Principal Malin called her name coming up the stairs.

She threw the children into the nearest empty room. "Wait here," she whispered. "And be still."

"Is that you?" Principal Malin said again. "Ah, yes!" He came from around the corner—the two strange men strangely behind him. "I thought I heard you. With whom were you speaking?" Miss Hope tried to speak, but Principal Malin cut her off. "No matter," he said. "I didn't see Arné nor Saturn downstairs. Have you perhaps seen them?"

"I haven't, no," Miss Hope breathed. "But, well, Sir, you know how many children there are. Maybe they hid among the others. Let me come with you and then—" she didn't get to finish again.

"Yes. Let's go and have another look, shall we," Principal Malin spoke though as if Miss Hope was the one in trouble. He turned around. "Are you coming?"

"Coming," Miss Hope said, signalling to Arné and Saturn to go down the other way as fast as their feet could carry them. "Right behind you, Malin."

It had taken them about five minutes to reach the cafeteria. Miss Hope had tried to stall them with either a too slow pace or making up some story about the rooms on their way. The cafeteria got nearer, and Miss Hope started to pray. A needle could have been heard as they entered. Every single child in that room, while waiting for their breakfast, came to an abrupt silence. All, Principal Malin and the two strange men, skimmed the room for Arné and Saturn. Principal Malin walked through the tables as every child he passed lowered their head in a terrified shame.

"Ah-ha," Principal Malin suddenly uttered. "There they are!" Arné and Saturn had managed to find their way into the cafeteria just in time. "Arné! Saturn!" he called them from the crowd of children. They approached him slowly in fear. "Can you be any slower!" He said irritated with the two strange men behind him. Miss Hope started to pray for the best. "Follow us," he spoke directly and turned around. "Carry on," he signalled for the children's breakfast.

Arné, Saturn, Miss Hope and the two strange men followed Principal Malin back into the house's central part. Through the corridors. Up the stairs. Until they reached his office where they all entered with each their own emotion. The room was dark, even within the brink of the passing daylight. It made Arné and Saturn think if it was only in their minds.

"What seems to be the problem?" Miss Hope asked curiously with concern.

"I'll tell you what the problem is," Principal Malin boasted as he walked impatiently up and down his office. "It seems that we have thieves in the house."

"What?" said Miss Hope.

"Yes," Principal Malin said and walked over to the two children and grabbed them by the shoulders. "And what is this," he said. "Wet."

"I can explain everything, sir," Arné suddenly uttered out of turn. Miss Hope tried to silence him. "It really is all my fault."

"No," Principal Malin shouted. "Not this time, you can't. But before I deal with that, I need to know something."

"What is the means of all this?" Miss Hope asked again.

Furiously, Principal Malin went to stand by the side of the two strange men. "Seems that someone has taken something that belonged to these men."

Arné, who knew well what Principal Malin was talking about, unlike Saturn and Miss Hope, took a step forward.

"The ring!" he screamed angrily. They had never seen him like this before.

"We don't have it," Saturn tried to explain, but Principal Malin had nothing of it.

He turned his attention towards Arné. "You know what I am talking about, don't you, Arné? You had told it to me yourself."

And by that movement and the words which had escaped his mouth he had, as it wasn't before, successfully changed the course of his timeline and how many more he did not know. "Yes, Sir," he said. "Please, Sir, if you'd only give me a chance to explain. It never belonged to—"

"Where is it?" Principal Malin shouted.

"In my room," Arné said as he looked towards Saturn's confused and betrayed face.

BOOK V

A Dream Re-dreamt

POV Saturn exc. 33 & 40

Chapter Thirty-Three

Left Someone Something

THE EVENTS OF THAT NIGHT appeared as though they were fused into one whole panorama of radical actions. Arné knew it would have eventually come to pass, yet his journal could not have prepared him for the experience per se. Although the house was well-lit, the night felt gloomy. And it came from an entire dreary day. For some unknown reason, both Arné and Saturn was held in solitary for the whole of the day, until Principal Malin and the two strange men had taken them back. The walls, which once formed a shelter, now collapsed on everything that stood in their way.

Why would Arné lie? Saturn thought. The ring was lost. Unless, of course, he had taken it. That made sense. Principal Malin thought it was with him.

"Please, Sir," Arné said once again in the office.

"I don't care!" Principal Malin shouted; his expressions looked the same. "Take him away at this instance. Take him to his room," he ordered the two strange men. "I knew, boy, the day you stepped through that door what devil is inside of you. And I regret above all ignoring my gut feeling about you."

"I really can explain," Miss Hope intervened. "If you would only give me a minute—a chance to explain."

But Principal Malin had none of it. He simply couldn't care less. And anything Miss Hope had said, would not get Arné out of trouble. Not tonight.

The men grabbed hold of Arné's upper arm. "No," he cried in his resistance. But the men were merely bigger and more durable than he was.

Observing the incidences, Saturn was paralysed by a pounding heart against the corner of the room. *Make it stop, make it stop, make it stop*, Saturn prayed. Miss Hope, who had just about enough of it, walked towards Arné to free him from the two men's grips. It was a struggle. And in Miss Hope's attempt, one of the men hit her with his elbow. It was a blow so hard that it caused her to fall to the ground.

"This is madness," she cried as Saturn rushed towards her side.

"Take him away!" Principal Malin shouted.

"You can't do this. This is insane. Who do you think you are? Have you gone out of your mind?" Miss Hope said and saw how Saturn left her side.

"One day you'll understand," Principal Malin said. And as he saw how Saturn tried to free Arné too, he continued. "Look now, how you have already corrupted this poor and innocent soul."

"Arné!" Saturn shouted, but one of the men let go of Arné and grabbed hold of Saturn. Ultimately pulling the two children from each other.

"Take that one to solitary. That'll fix it up," Principal Malin said to the man holding Saturn.

"Arné!"

"Saturn!"

Those were the words they shouted as they were breathtakingly dragged away from each other down the hall to the moment they couldn't see each other anymore.

Miss Hope felt a deep cut in her soul as she was but forced to merely observe the events which had taken place that evening; a brutal emotional pruning she would never come to recover from. It seems the moon had almost lost its brightness within its ever oppression of reflecting light upon the darkness of this world—a night which now took over. Darkness, nothing can prepare you for. And the children of the orphanage, who all lay silently in their rooms, were too afraid to come out for they could hear the arguments coming from every hall.

Saturn's eyes swelled. The black door down to solitary got nearer. And though Saturn's arm started to bruise from the tight clutch of the man, and though Saturn complained, "Please let me go, you're hurting me," the man but returned in silence and his hand stiff. It was a green mile of endless suffer down to a hell Saturn had once only feared.

The next sound the man did cause was that coming from the door as he kicked it open. A chilly wind, with the scent of cement, suddenly hit both their faces. Half a dozen wooden steps were fixed to a brick wall supported by a metal structure. No handrail. And the pendant light, hanging from the ceiling, blown. But as the man had kicked the door open, in a forgetful rage, he let go a little of his grasp, and Saturn saw an only chance to escape before all hell breaks loose. So, with one blow coming from deep down somewhere inside, one strike with every weight, Saturn pushed the man. The wooden steps hammered as he fell down them. And without even bothering to witness the event, Saturn rushed back to Arné's dorm. Something which seemed like another mile. Saturn was halfway through when an unexpected hand caught grip of Saturn's back.

"Running around now," the cook said. "Shouldn't you be in bed?"

"Please, Sir," Saturn looked up, "you don't understand. I need to get to Arné."

"No need," he said. "Let's get you to Malin's office."

"No Sir, they are in Arné's room."

The cook looked confused. And so with his grip on Saturn, they proceeded to the dorm. It was almost too late when they finally arrived. And though every thought about the worst outcome to the night had flashed right in front of Saturn's very eyes, a strange sense of fight had sprung in Saturn's heart – something unusual coming from Saturn.

Miss Hope stood behind Principal Malin, who was blocking the now empty dorm room entrance. That was, apart from the other strange man who had just thrown Arné down onto the floor. *The children of the dorm must have been chased away*; Saturn assumed.

"It is an abomination!" Principal Malin shouted. "I see the evil of his doings—sinner!"

Miss Hope attempted to enter the room when Principal Malin stopped her and pushed her away. She fell to the ground. "We're born into sin; we aren't born with it!" she exclaimed and then looked over and saw the cook. "Faith, please. I know there's a good man inside of you. Help us."

Principal Malin had none of it. He glanced at an oil lamp in his irrational thought and emotion; it stood on a cupboard next to the door. "Burn! Burn like you'll burn in hell, my boy!" he said as he pushed it over.

Faith looked on. As harsh as he was, he couldn't believe his own two eyes. "Malin!" he shouted. "What on earth is going on here?"

Saturn looked on in disbelief; it started to feel like a dream. It couldn't be real. This strange sensation, though like a nightmare in which your five senses functioned, and yet also hope that everyone will soon wake from it.

"No!" Miss Hope cried an offset for Saturn's sprint, passing her.

And again, with every little bit of strength left, Saturn pushed Principal Malin into the room. He fell against the strange man pushing him over as well. "Come!" Saturn reached out to Arné.

And just as the two wanted to exit the room, the strange man grabbed onto Saturn's ankle, leaving Saturn to trip and fall. Arné looked back as Saturn fell headfirst onto one of the bed knobs. The blow was hard, ultimately leaving Saturn unconscious.

Faith made haste, picking Saturn up and as he exited the room, Arné shut the door with immense force, breaking off the handle as he did and leaving the door locked without intention. He helped Miss Hope to her feet. The smoke had quickly reached the other dormitories, leaving signal for the children to run. And so they did. They quickly caught up with Arné, Miss Hope and Faith who carried Saturn outside.

It was something like a dream for Arné as well. Maybe even something more profound and darker, something that left him speechless as he looked on over the burning house with all the other children running outside and waiting for help. He had gotten burnt too in the room, without even noticing it. Only then the sting returned. A bite that will rest with him forever. But the pain was not so bad, something he felt like he could endure, but when Arné thought about the fire, and all that got lost now with it, that sting felt worse. For there in the midst still lay his journal. And in that journal his letter. Sirens quickly came from that old town: police, ambulances, fire department, locals. Many had come – not all to help though. None of the children were seriously injured that night, apart from Arné and Saturn of course. Miss Hope had gone with both of them to the hospital that night. Arné was lucky enough to have been discharged the next morning, but Saturn was unfortunately not that lucky.

"Do you want to say goodbye to Saturn, Arné?" Miss Hope asked him that morning as two social workers who came to pick him up stood behind him. "He may, may he not?" she quickly glanced at them.

"Of course," one of them said.

And as Arné stood with tears in his eyes – as he told himself not to cry, he needs to stay healthy-looking at his most beloved friend lying still on the bed, he took Saturn's hand. "I'm sorry, Sats. I really am. I didn't mean for any of this to have happened. I promise," he said, and as the social workers escorted him from the room, he quickly ran back. "I'll be looking for you," he whispered. "Please remember me."

Arné didn't speak much after that morning. He didn't speak at all, in fact. And as he sat in the backseat of the car, watching the social workers trying to keep him calm and going over the procedure, he looked from the window. And the last thing he heard when he went into his own little world was that the woman, they are taking

him to is genuinely kind. Her name is Miss Precious, and she had signed up to help as a fostering parent.
As for Saturn, who had woken up a few days later with severe amnesia, Saturn had come to stay with Miss Hope as a foster parent.

Chapter Thirty-Four

Chronology

IT WAS A BEAUTIFUL THING to have witnessed: the disappearance of a conscious mind. It gave me a glimpse of what was waiting for me when I shall finally return. For then, too, my spirit shall drift off like butterflies made from pure stardust. I stood still. Arné was gone. And as I glanced over the mountain towards the moon, my eyes lowered. The mountain stayed unmoved. The moon reflected over the lake. Arné's clothes in my hands. I stared on with disbelieve. I walked back slowly. Pensively. Incredulously. Until I reached the house and found Sneaky awaited my arrival impatiently, signifying it with a swift cry, though as if he knew.

"He's gone, buddy." I didn't believe my own speech. Sneaky lowered his head disinterested as I lay Arné's clothes down in front of him and lowered myself. I patted his head as my own fear for dogs had disappeared. And there I waited at a loss.

Sneaky's ears suddenly lifted. I knew the next thing was a vibration coming from the clothes I had put down a moment ago. I took a look.

Arné's phone, I thought and picked it up.

"Hi, buddy," Joy spoke lively. "Just wanted to know if everything's alright. You never messaged me back."

I could not bring myself to speak.

"Arné?"

I made a soft cry as I tried to speak. "Joy."

"Saturn?" he said. "What's wrong?"

"He's gone. Arné is gone."

I could hear over the phone that he was startled by the news. And without putting the phone down, I dropped it, with the final words coming from the earpiece: "We are on our way – hang on – don't worry," and fainting at the same time.

I remembered the next thing was opening my eyes blinded by the brink of sunlight throwing itself in by the house's windowpanes. I was out for the entire night.

Grace's image emerged slowly through the blinding of the light. "Hey," she said, her hand caressing my leg as Sneaky's warm breath heaved against the other leg. I started to cry directly, of course, I did. "Don't worry," she said. "We are here now."

A week after that day, I found myself back in New City, living with my brother. Jupiter was never a spiteful person. And he had never brought up his initial concern, that one day after Arné's passing, I'll be alone.

Instead, he comforted me. And inspired me to endure. "Hold on Saturn," he said to me once. "And know that there will come a time you shall see him again." He spoke the truth. When I think back, I believe that I would have gotten lost if it wasn't for him.

And a month after that day, I found myself again, living the habitual life I had lived before. Stand up – work – Miss Hope – sleep. Though there were occasional variations to this. Recreation and population had not left me depressed. Yet, within all that was said, there was a change. I had found what I had sought for. There was no need to look for any answers anymore. I knew the answer to my original and initial question.

So, on the first day, I went back to Miss Hope for our daily rendezvous, I told her everything that had happened. The good and the bad. And I tried not to leave out too much detail. I wanted her to know everything. "And that's what happened while I was gone," I concluded my story that late afternoon as I stared into those same hollow eyes, I had looked at one year ago. Miss Hope was still unaware. "You would've been proud of Arné. He had become an extraordinary man."

Into the bargain, I do not ever wish to recall the decades which came to pass after Arné's first passing. As it was, the time I had with Arné was incredible, that in comparison, the years after had struck me in their gravest form of insignificance. Well, as it was, populated and congenial in their own sense. It was worth mentioning that Joy and Grace had spent the rest of their lives at the manor and worked at the coffee house. I had moved into my own apartment in New City, where I taught music for the remainder of my years. Jupiter, Verity and Happiness were there too.

In fact, I did go back to that house very often, but it reminded me too much of him, and I grew too impatient for his return when I was there. The house was his legacy. That one thing he left me as he knew his own fate.

We were all old now and with that age had come more loss and memories. I had sojourned through Miss Hope's death and that of Sneaky's and many others until it was finally my turn to go.

The hospital smelled of strong cleaning detergent and medicine and enclosed a cold death sensation in the air. I do remember feeling quite lonely when I had first gotten here, Joy and Grace could not stay for long periods of time, and close friends were either passed on or had forgotten about my existence. Still, the personnel had made me feel very comfortable, spoiled me with extra pudding and took me for walks in the open air.

In that time, I often wondered about the relationships of other people, and I asked whether Arné and mine were supremely different from theirs, even without the time constraint. It made me feel lucky in a sense when I saw how many of them also broke only after one small disagreement, that I had known life in good fortune towards love.

And so, as I lay on my deathbed like I had lived those days, biding my time to return to – ironically – that house which had yet again found a way back into my life, it came with the sullen movement of my eyes closing in on my death.

Chapter Thirty-Five

Turning Back the Clock-Wheel

FOR YEARS I HAD PONDERED over the sentiment of reaction upon my return. But it was not until my eyes had opened all those years back – that I found myself in a state of an abundance of immense mixed emotion, which had brought tears to my eyes – that I got to feel the sensation; as strange as it may sound, of learning a new passion. And like a phoenix, he had risen from his own ashes, and as I glanced onto his light, I had done something. Something so irrefutable, so impulsive, that upon its imminent arrival, not even Arné would be able to turn back. I chose to forget. I decided to ignore how it will all come to pass.

And so, before he could say a word, I mounted him. "You're back! You're here! I can't believe it." I said. "It's really you," I whispered as his heartbeat pounded against mine.

I heard Grace and Joy in the background with their confusing whispers about what was happening.

"Do you think it actually worked?" Grace whispered to Joy.

"I don't know," he answered. "They look the same to me."

"Well, I don't think that it'll change them physically."

"I don't know," Joy said again.

Arné lifted my chin up as we sat up straight. "How long has it been?" he whispered.

"Fifty years," I replied, though the number was higher.

Arné looked at me though as if he had broken a promise that in a sense, he had left me behind, done me wrong. "I'm sorry," he cried.

So, I placed my hands on his face and silenced his cry. "That's okay. It's not your fault," I said.

"So… Did it work?" Grace whispered. It made us smile within the sadness we felt, that – by the look on his face – he too felt a sense of happiness.

I glanced over towards Grace. "It worked," I said, "this is our second time." We remained on the floor, though as if we were exhausted from running a marathon.

Joy was relieved to hear that. I could see it in his eyes. Though his warning was correct all along, and Arné and I did not know it then, we were about to face an inevitable event.

"So, what happened?" Joy asked curiously.

I looked back at Arné still in regret and smiled, trying to make him feel better. "I'd rather not say," I said. "Let's retake it step-by-step."

And that was what we did.

"So," Arné said unexpectedly, "shall we celebrate our return?"

I nodded with a smile and almost with tears in my eyes. "Yes," I said. "What shall we do?"

Grace suddenly looked up. "What about the beach?"

"Perfect," Joy sounded relieved. For he had, a moment ago, bargained for the worst to happen. "We have some champagne. We can make a bonfire and celebrate there."

We loaded the car and headed straight to the beach. There we enjoyed each other's company within the forefront of waves crashing.

With our camping chairs packed around the fire and champagne in our hand, Joy made the first toast. "Good fortune."

"To family," said Grace.

"To seconds," said Arné.

"To love," I said.

Grace and Arné took a walk together on the beach after our toasts. And it was a perfect time to ask Joy something. Something that still bothered me since the day it started.

"Joy," I started. "I wanted to speak to you," I said grateful for the opportunity to talk to him alone.

"Yes," he answered.

"I know that Arné will not ask you this. I don't think it's because of his pride, but I think he'll be too afraid to ask you."

His smile turned into concern. "What happened?"

"When we did this the first time around, Arné and I had skipped a month because he forgot that he had already lived it." I must lie if I say I wasn't scared to tell him about it too. But I pulled through. "Do you think—?" I didn't know how to ask it, but fortunately, he understood what I implied.

"I see," he said pensively. He didn't turn. Instead, he remained calm and thought about the implications. "I don't know what to say. But I can't see how it can harm you too much. I wouldn't be too concerned about it. If you have to go through it alone, Grace and I will still be here for you." He tried to calm me.

"Hey, what are you guys talking about?" Grace said upon their return.

"Can ask you guys the same thing," Joy joked.

Arné came to give me a kiss. "Everything good?"

"Yeah," I said. "Why?"

"Just asking," he grinned and kissed me again.

Soon after that, as the fire burned out, we returned home as well.

That night we made love again. For the first time in years. Though our passion had appeared differently. We have made love before, yet it felt not so; it was as if we made love again; for the first time, our minds knew it, our bodies did not. I was a virgin that first time. I knew he wasn't. Whether it was with me in another timeline or someone completely different that time, he went rogue. But his love for and towards me made me reconcile. His attitude proved that I was the one he loved. And still, till now, I remembered how safe I felt afterwards. For like always, he was there the following morning.

So, the next morning, Earnest and Verity had joined us for, what was supposed to be a brief hello, a sociable lunch. We had discussed the house and renovations all over again. For the house was back in its original state. Otherwise, when I thought back to it, I couldn't help but wonder why it was when I first heard Alina's name, what significance it had implied for me. Though like change.

So it was that we started our second time living the year. And even if I have to say it myself, I couldn't have asked for better second inception. It was yet ominous, though when I thought about it. For it was though as if Arné and I could see into the future. We knew what was about to happen. And we could change how we wanted to live it like we chose to go to the beach. However, there remained some things unchanged. Things that were still out of our reach like Earnest and Verity's surprise visit.

Chapter Thirty-Six

―――――

A Golden Age

THE YEAR WHICH FOLLOWED WAS admittedly a golden age. Though as if we had gotten a second chance together.

There were rivers of gold:

By its peculiar circumstance, we were yet defined by our surroundings. As it was, in Arné and my minds, we were already married, but not according to those of the people surrounding us. And so we had gotten married again, though sooner than before. We also still had conversations as we had back then, like telling Jupiter and Serenity all about the year we were living, or Grace wanting to celebrate our succession. We did all the usual things set in a year, again like birthdays and holidays. And we amused ourselves with the beach and city.

We built a city of gold:

As it was, the house was back in the state in which it had first appeared when I saw it. And so we went ahead with the renovations all over again. It struck me though that in another timeline, my life will continue in others' minds, though I, in my mind, won't. And this will be the place Joy and Grace, and Arné and I will find ourselves all over again. The house amused my thoughts though; for in its truth – it never haunted us – it was, in a strange way, Arné and I who had always managed to find ourselves here. And even within all its ruins, we ever came back to it. If not anything, it was a great symbol of love – where two souls, once broken, were fixed. It was home now.

There were treasures of gold:

Arné read to me again, and I played him the piano. And then there was the intimacy between us which had blossomed like a rose in spring. And yet also, like the first time when we had made love, nothing had made me feel so safe as to know that he would be lying with me in bed till the next morning. Sneaky was another golden treasure, ironically, being a golden retriever.

There were also things not so golden:

As it was, we had to endure Faith's death all over again. We did try to prevent it from happening, though. And we asked them to go and see a doctor. But still, it had not worked. Faith had a heart attack in the hospital and died there. It made me think about time in a new light. For if it's your time, it's your time. This included Patience leaving at the end. Still, I remember the first time she told me about Faith. One of the only things I've learned of my past by someone else's accounts and not by memory. He was the cook of the orphanage back when Arné and I still stayed there. He had changed though, by some mysterious event that had taken place there one night, Patience told me. Yet he never spoke about it here.

I also told Arné about the fifty years which had come after my life with him. Though it wasn't sad – and maybe even golden in its own sense – it was something I had to bear without him.

The last least golden thing was the memory of my brother I had gotten. It happened one unexpected morning. I woke up, and by the noise going around the orphanage house, I could tell that something was wrong.

"It's your brother," one of the other kids in my dorm said to me as I still woke up.

"What!" I shouted and ran downstairs, out front the main entrance, almost trembling down the stairs as I did. All, still wearing my pyjamas.

The incident was halfway through - coming to a close. I was too late. Jupiter was already put in a car as I came out. And Principal Malin looked on with a smirk all over his face. The cab's back window was lowered, and his head stuck out as he saw me.

"Jupiter!" I shouted as I ran up to the car. My hand touching his as he stuck it out. I grabbed hold of it as tightly as I could. Then I felt a grip from behind. Principal Malin tried to take me away. "Don't leave me," I shouted. "Jupiter!"

"Go now!" Principal Malin shouted to the driver.

"Jupiter!" I cried as my hand felt untouched, Principal Malin holding me behind.

Principal Malin did not procrastinate in telling me why my brother was taken away. That very instant, he took my shoulder, looked me in the eye, and explained it to me. "Your brother is a bad person," he indoctrinated me to believe what he said was actually true. "There is something inside of your brother, Saturn. Something I don't want you to catch. It will be better if you just forget about him."

I ran away. Straight to Miss Hope. She comforted me all day long, and that evening, she took me to her chambers in secret. We sat on her bed as she opened her bedside drawer and took something from it.

"Saturn," she said. "Just before your brother left, he had given me something. He asked me to give it to you."

"What is it?" I asked curiously.

"Give me your hand," she said, and as I did, she placed the artefact in my palm and closed it.

I put my hand near my chest and opened it again. And there lay the ring in the palm of my hand. Safe.

"You must keep it safe," she explained. "And not tell anybody of it."

I nodded.

I thought that she would have kept it herself, to keep guard over it, if she could, but it was not hers. And as my brother was just taken away from me, she must have thought that I needed something to remember him by—something to make me feel close to him.

And though when I had gotten the memory, I had not known what it meant. It will be that soon after I'd remembered it, that the meaning shall become clear in revelations.

Chapter Thirty-Seven

Dissolution

LIKE ALL THINGS, THAT GOLDEN age had come to an end as well. One morning, I woke up, and I knew that something was wrong, even out of place, and the sullen silence which lurked throughout the house substantiated it. Arné was gone.

At first, I tried to deny it, and unknown of its severity and the first thing I did was, I ran downstairs with the hopes of finding Arné below preparing us breakfast—he wasn't. Neither were the kitchenware. And when I had come to realise that I suddenly, with a blow to my head, realised the house was dark and swept clean of any household supplies. I wasn't wearing my pyjamas and had come to think of it, I didn't wake up on a bed. The event had left me dumbstruck to fullness, and I fell to the ground with my body leaning against a wall. And so, I did the one thing – I think most people would have done in a comparable situation – I waited. Telling myself that I was dreaming. That Arné will show up. That everything will go back to normal.

By the time night had fallen, I was faced with the undefined truth, that he will not show up and everything will stay as it is.

Suddenly I heard a phone ringing. I moved abruptly about, figuring out where the sound was coming from until I found it in an empty room.

"Hello," I answered. And to my amazement, a once-familiar voice answered back.

"Hello, Honey."

"Miss Hope," I said, confused.

"Yes," she said. "Is everything okay?"

"I don't understand," I said. "I'm at the house and he—"

She cut me off. "Oh, my dear. I know. It gets me down too to think Arné's not with us anymore. Still till this day. But come home please."

Dumbstruck, I ended the call. And as I did, it was though as if the ruins in which that house had lain was of great aid, for I had remembered my last memory. The memory that completed the whole of my past.

The more I remembered, the more I did realise that this town had a well-kept secret. So concealed that only a few therein had knowledge of its mystery. We all have secrets (I assume), and I do not think it is anybody else's goal in life to find you. I think, on the contrary, it is our own purpose in life to recognise our own.

But the memory of what had happened that night in the orphanage house was a great revelation. The two strange men I had once seen was not real. How could they be as I now saw they died that night in the fire with Principal Malin right before I hit my head? They were, though, as I saw now the mere manifestation from my own mind trying to tell me what had happened. And they were, in a sense the manifestation representation of time and death. And it now seemed that this dissolution was an offset case: reminding me of the one thing I had once cared for most in this world, and that was knowledge. And though I had it now, nothing could prepare me for what was about to happen during the next month.

And as I got my last memory of my life. I thought. I never wanted Arné to tell me anything, and I saw now why it was so difficult for him to tell me what had happened. But still, the experience of remembering was worth it.

I was as well, as it was, face-to-face with the one thing Joy had once warned us about – stuck within a butterfly effect of our own doings, experienced to its extreme. I didn't know which was worse: being alone or being confused; and overwhelmed, I fainted.

That following morning, I woke up to yet other familiar voices in the vastness of the house. "Hello?" I felt a bump on the shoulder.

I looked up, and as I tried to stand up with his helping hand and spoke his name, so I have raised confusion on his face. "Joy," I said.

At first, he remained still and silent, though as if he had thought I was someone else. "Yes?" He didn't' say anything else.

"Look at you," another familiar voice said standing beside me. "Is everything alright?"

"Grace," I said. I raised as much confusion in her as in Joy.

They looked at each other for a moment. And I am confident that by the judge of my outfit, I knew I wasn't some homeless person who sought shelter.

"Can we get you something to eat? Or drink? Can we call someone for you?" Grace said concerningly.

I was still very much confused. Even more, than all of them, me certainly. "Arné is…" I said dumbstruck. "How are you two here?"

"Sorry, I don't understand," Joy said, "do you know us?"

I didn't reply.

"Let's get you something to eat," Grace said. "You'll feel better then."

We went into town and found ourselves in the same Coffee House I used to work at.

"Saturn," Patience greeted us by the door. "My word, what happened? Come and sit down."

I made some excuse that I wasn't feeling well and Patience brought us things to eat. When I explained to Joy and Grace what had happened, Joy took it better than Grace.

"Why were you at the house?" I asked.

"I actually lost my brother in there," Joy explained. "Grace came with me to see where he grew up. I never knew him, though. My mom had put him up for adoption. Tragedy what happened isn't it. To die like that. Being burned to death. Anyway, my mom just told me the other day." Joy and Arné were brothers.

The following month, I stayed with Faith and Patience and worked in the coffee house. I visited the house every time I could. Coming to terms with, what I was sure of now, that he had died in another reality.

Chapter Thirty-Eight

Keeper of Time

THE INCOHERENCY OF THAT HOUSE had a tie on me; something I felt was a sense of attraction. Almost like a whisper. Something calling me back time after time again. By the end of that month, I had come to visit the house more times I could remember, which was inexplicable as there were only so many days in a month, hence only so many days I could have gone to visit it. But, yet in my mind, it felt like water over a rock.

I found myself again there amid its ruins. I walked over the burned skeleton of the house, though as if I was a forensic investigator. I searched for some unknown answer, though I did not even have the question, to begin with. But my eyes were like that of a hawk's; they never stopped searching. And, alas, out of the corner of my eye, something had caught my attention.

I walked over to the spot and dusted off a book as I picked it up. It was burnt black, though the pages seemed still intact. But as I had picked it up, an envelope burned at its side had fallen out. I picked it up and went over to a clean spot where I could sit and read. Placing the book to my side, I opened the envelope first and pulled out a letter burnt similarly than the envelope:

Dear Saturn Love,

May, in hope, this find you well, my love; wherever you might
wander about in time.

I dreamed about you last night, set inside my mother's womb;
though as if there is a holiness to the closure of our fates.
And I will hard to lie if I'd say that I haven't dreamt
about you every day since. Sometimes even chafe until dusk
to do. And even then before I close my eyes, I often wonder
about the stars and wish that if only I could have but
one authentic day with you, also set in the coldest of
winter days, I could make summer reflect in our heart's
affections, just like the moon. There are many things, my love,
I had come to know, but it was your love I ever needed—
even by my own standards — for your love is the alloy of
the pain of any savageness and brutality.

For within a perfect world, my love, we would have found
each other, hence for that world, I shall strive. But
if I should have come to fail and not succeeded in
my own chance at ends, I only wish that I had played
my part well in love. And you, my love, by the time
you shall read this - like it is the intention of any
such letter - I won't be there with you.

But you can always find me, find me and meet
me there!

Let's set forth to the great green hills, my love.
Let's set forth whence the mountain greets the sky
And cries the lake beneath damon's lonely eye.
Let's set forth thence to be for our behove.

Yours forever truly,
Aimé Vichie

I love you.

P.S.   I'm looking for you.

By the time I had finished reading, tears were already rolling down my cheeks. My feet had already come to hurry one after the other over the ground underneath them. I made my way to the lakeside. The book was in my right hand as well, and I stopped by the lake's view as the wind hurried over my shoulders.

The letter, set outside of its own context, didn't make sense to me. Yet even there I felt though as if Arné was trying to tell me something. Something deep. Something he couldn't put down in words. Still, the simplest of phrases from the letter kept on running inside of my mind in question. "Wherever you might wonder about in time."

How did you know?

"I'm looking for you."

Why?

"But you can always find me; find me and meet me there!"

"Where?" I asked him in his absence. It must have gone on for some time when suddenly the book in my hand alerted itself by its weight. I opened it. And from its writing, I made it out as a type of diary.

for within a perfect world we would
have found each other; hence for
that world, I shall strive!

Hello. (c.a. 53)
Who is this?

Hello, Arné. My name is also Arné, what a coincidence, am I
right? I got you this diary a few years back. Do you like
it? (c.a. 55)
It's okay, I guess. What do you mean by also Arné?

I will explain everything to you. But first I need you to
promise me something. (c.a. 57)
What?

I need you to read this diary every day to see if I've
written to you. It's very important. (c.a. 59)
I'll try... What do you mean by that...? "It's important."
And what's up with this c.a. crap???

It's important because something very bad can happen
if you don't. (c.a. 59)
Like what? How do you know? c.a.?

Well, you see these things are all connected because
I am from the future and c.a. is how old I am.
And I know something bad will happen because I
have already seen it. (c.a. 59)
Who are you?

I am you, Arné. (c.a. 59)
Prove it!

> Let's set forth to the great green hills, my love.
> Let's set forth whence the mountain greets the sky
> And aries the lake beneath dawn's lonely eye.
> Let's set forth thence to be for our behove.
>
> (c.a. 59)

I wrote that! Stalker! how do you know about that only Saturn knows it Saturn this is you I mean, Saturn didn't know anything about this.

No... Because we wrote it. (c.a. 59)

What will happen?   What bad I mean? (c.a. 15)

Now, Arné, I need you to read this very carefully because what I am about to write to you is very very important. (c.a. 59)

I'm reading... (c.a. 15)

There will have to be a few things you'll need to do:
1. You need to go to Principal Malin and tell him that you can travel in time. ✓ (c.a. 15)
2. I need you to get Saturn's ring without Saturn noticing anything. ✓ (c.a. 15)
3. I need you to show Saturn a day in the future
4. When you see two strange men lurking around

the house, you'll know that the time is near. Let me know when you see them. ✓ (c.a. 15)

(c.a. 59)

What will happen if I can't do all of these things? (c.a. 15)

I'm afraid someone can get hurt badly. (c.a. 59)

Hurt badly how? And tell the truth! (c.a. 15)

A murder will be committed tomorrow evening in the orphanage house. The body of the child will be found near the orphanage house by the lake side surrounded by the mountain and hills. Saturn will be the one who dies. (c.a. 59)

I don't understand? (c.a. 15)

What do you not understand? (c.a. 59)

I did 1 and 2, But I didn't need to do 2 because Saturn doesn't have a ring. I have a ring though... pink and brownish. And why tell P.M. that I can travel in time? Can you travel in time? Can I travel in time? What do you mean by ~~telling~~ showing Saturn a day in the future? The men showed up today. What must I do ??? (c.a. 15)

Please help! I can't sleep. I'm scared (c.a. 15)

That's okay. I'm going to tell you a secret. I also get

It had me by the throat. All of it. From the memory of that night to the letter I read, to the very last sentence on that page. And though I was at a loss at this stage, just like a mouse stuck in an endless maze of hoops, there wasn't going to be any other question nor answer coming from that diary. For, page after page lay in the clear. There was nothing else written down in that diary apart from that conversation. But it did make me see the connectedness of our lives.

But it did make me realize something. Arné had communicated with himself. Whatever difficulty that had held or the complexity of the thought. And yet, he had managed to do so. And I remembered seeing him writing to himself when we were younger, and it made me think if it had so occurred that he wrote to himself in a state of dream-writing.

After my senses had started to resurface again – and though it was difficult in the beginning, it got more comfortable as time went on – my line of thought got clear. Four things went through my mind at that time. The first was Joy and Arné's relationship, and though I didn't know why Arné never told him that he was, in fact, his brother, I thought it had something to do with Arné being put up for adoption.

What had happened that night in the orphanage was the second thing that went through my mind. I now understood that there is more to his story than what I had initially thought. And yet he may have died in this timeline, I wondered in how many more he must have tried to save me and at ends had succeeded.

The letter was third. Arné knew that we will have been separated by the end of that night, and I knew that he wanted to give me that letter, and though he had not succeeded, I now understood why. He tried to tell me that he's looking. In a way, asking me to wait for him. Yet, I felt something more profound in connection, though as if he wanted to tell me more. Something he couldn't just spit out of his mouth or portray on a piece of paper.

Finally, I thought about the diary and how many more of its kind was out there. Though this one hadn't given me a lot of answers, I couldn't help but wonder if there was one. One that would explicitly tell you everything.

But as I wondered about the answers, it *did* give me a sense of certainty that there was in fact, something more to his life that had come to me. Though as if I had all the dots but the links were missing. I knew that the two strange men were after the ring. And the ring was in my possession. Yet, in this reality, it was not. Arné told himself that he owned the ring, which did not make sense at all. Why would he had had the ring? Did that have something to do with him back then in the other reality, not knowing that he could travel in time?

I started to walk around in circles in order the think more clearly. And as I passed that big rock, I found Arné's old fishing rod. It was rusted and lay next to the moss growing on the rock. I picked it up and walked over to the lake again.

I started wondering for a couple of minutes when a new memory presented itself to me.

Arné and I were here by the lake talking as we usually had. He was on the rock with the fishing rod, and I stood next to the foundation with the wavelets crushing over my two bare feet.

"Do you think one can go to the future to change the past?" he asked me. And I could remember staggering over that question, for it had not made any sense to me.

"What do you mean?" I asked.

He was in a pensive mood. "I don't know," he said, "if you were never born but still existing does that make you... I don't know... alive. But you exist, though. So... can you go to your future to make sure you'll be born?"

He was speaking in circles; I could remember that. But I could not make sense of his questions. "Arné," I said, "if you are here, then that must surely mean that you are alive." I climbed up onto the rock and hugged him tightly from behind. "See... I wouldn't have been able to just do that if you weren't."

The fishing rod fell to the ground from the grasp of my hand. "You were never born," I said to myself enlighteningly. Though it was but only presented as pieces, the complete puzzle has always been there inside of my mind. It waited patiently to be fixed together. And yet, now, I was stuck with a new question. *How do I save you, Arné?*

Once again, my thoughts were scrambled, and I decided to look at the envelope one more time. And there it was. As I emptied the envelope, the ring fell from it onto my left hand. And as I regarded it, picking it up with my right, I couldn't help but notice that it was altered.

For inside the ring there stood: "*Like a candle under the water.*"

And as I read the writing, I thought about Jupiter and the day he was taken away from me. That night Arné went to tell Principal Malin about his secret, and I couldn't help but recognize the similarities between the two cases. As I recall Principal Malin's words to Arné: "I've dealt with one of you once before." And it all made sense. For in the context Principal Malin had spoken, he referred to Jupiter as he told me that day Jupiter was taken away from me: "There's something inside your brother, Saturn. Something I don't want you to catch."

Jupiter was able to travel in time. And that I had not seen, nor linked these two events together was dazzling. Nevertheless, I set out to Jupiter that exact same day – for I knew I needed to get to him; I needed to get there fast – and so I arrived at New Town the following morning on my bus.

I needed to be honest when I said that I didn't know what to expect. I didn't know much about my timeline's events, except that Miss Hope was still alive and healthy; I had stayed with her for who knows how long. But concerning Jupiter, nothing. Not even if he knew me. So, when I finally did find him, in front of his and Serenity's suburban home, mowing his lawn, and the moment he saw me, he gave me a hug and said: "Saturn. Where have you been?" I could remember he would speak to calm everyone and everything around him in that same kind voice. I almost burst out in tears.

"You wouldn't believe me if I tell you," though I did know he would be able to relate.

He quickly took me into the house and prepared us both a cup full of tea to relax me, and I told him everything. "I also know now why you couldn't' tell me all about your childhood with mom and dad and me," I said to the end of my story. "And I also know why you were taken away from me all those years back when we were still at the orphanage house."

He looked at me with silence.

"You can travel in time too," I said.

Jupiter sighed, and with one exhaling breath, he said, "Yes."

I took his hand.

"I travelled in time and saw our fates. And I had not lived my youth for I wish to see Mom and Dad again in my last days."

He looked sad and pensive. And now that I knew the truth, I didn't know how to ask of him what I wanted to ask of him. Will he save Arné? I took out the ring in my pocket, and I placed it on the kitchen counter where we stood.

"I can still feel him... Searching... Wondering in time... Looking for me in some alien life," I said.

And just as I wanted to continue, he cut me off in that gentle voice of his. "You want me to save him," he said and reached for the ring as he placed a finger on it.

"There is something I hadn't told you."

"I'm listening."

"I died in that fire originally. And Arné had gone back in time to save me. So, if I do not get to save him to save me, I will have died. And will die now. So, I do not know how to ask of you such a thing. But yes. Yes, please, Jupiter. I love him." And I laid a photo of his mother on the table so he would know what she looks like, and I told him where he was born.

He sighed again. "It's done."

I was still getting used to it. For though Jupiter had travelled in time just a second ago, what felt for him like years had felt for me like a split second. "But how?" I asked him.

And he told me that when he had travelled in time just now, he had found the ring in his pocket in an attractive way and asked his parents to go to the hospital. When he found Arné's mother, he had given her a ring and told her that the ring belongs to Arné. She had not aborted Arné that day, for now, he had a piece of belonging. And she couldn't take from the child and instead put the child up for adoption, which resulted in him ending up and the same orphanage house Jupiter and Saturn went to.

And so, the ring had finally found its real keeper. He has always been the timekeeper. He has always been my keeper. And that Jupiter had saved him now. He had managed to go to his future to change his past. And though it does sound impossible, for it should have been – the past is in the past and should remain, so it doesn't even matter what you make people believe in other stories, and though you can't change it, you can choose to forgive and move on – Arné had managed to do it. For he had cheated time. He must have died by abortion, but his solo action – the action of wandering in time – had saved him – he made it possible for himself to live a healthy life. And the effect of travelling in time had given the ability to Jupiter – I thought – to do the same for Time had to make way for Arné to live. I went to bed, pondering over all that had happened.

Chapter Thirty-Nine

———

Agricultural

THE EXPERIENCE OF THE TRUTH was imponderable. That is why, when I woke up one following morning back in that same bed, I had gotten used to, I told Arné everything. And I do not think it well to recall any other of the day's events, for there lurks something genuine and unique and intimate about love, that sometimes, like a sensitive secret one does not share. But if I should say, it was at ends a delight to both our heart's affections.

However, I feel I must say that we had mysteriously found ourselves by the lake bank where we laid in each other's company by the final minutes of the day. I had asked him then about the ring and what happened to it; as he explained that the minute Jupiter had wandered with it through time – as it couldn't have been duplicated – it had disappeared from every timeline it had once endured and found itself anew.

But still, even in my own mind, I couldn't make sense of it. But Arné took my hand. "My love," he said, "it is not something to make sense of, it is something to believe," and then placed the ring in my hand.

As I glanced upon the artefact, it made me revere of that old legend Miss Hope had always told me about. The one about Saturn's rings. And it made me think. The ring didn't have any form of superpower, just like the one here didn't have any as well. In fact, the mere representation of it gave it its significance, which gave it love. He was finally cured of his curse.

Then, "look," he said. And as my gaze fell from the stars onto the big rock near the lake. And mystically, two rings which weren't there a moment before were now carved into it. We had for a brief moment wandered in time – to the near future – where once long ago in a distant past we both had walked to this day which Arné wanted to show me so that he would be able to find me once he looked for me. And a moment before we both parted our different ways as we gazed back onto the stars and then locked our lips, our eyes had closed again for one last time.

"Why did you choose me, even within the certainty of the uncertainty that I'll be able to save your life?" I asked as I saw now, he had the ring.

"My love," he said, "I didn't. How could I have chosen if there weren't any other to choose over from? There are more possibilities for the outcome of one's life than grains of sand on the earth's surface. And although I had only lived a friction of those lives, I had come to search for you endlessly, in all of them. Never stopping."

What a life he had executed, orchestrated it to the finest of details, now harvesting his crops, I thought.

Chapter Forty

From Left to Right – The Orchestrator

IN ARNÉ'S MIND, HE HAD this idea: that although he had lived so many lives, they were not real. For he was never truly born. That he had lived so many lives, but he had not taken part in his one actual reality. That to do so, he needed to save himself from something he had once believed was impossible. And yet, with that knowledge, he still kept Saturn. And in doing so, he devoted himself. He knew that now, as he looked at Saturn holding the ring and opened a letter in hand. It was, as it was, from left to right. A change of a full definition. Something new. Something better. It was like inexplicable magic—a miracle. And as he regarded the letter which had vanished into mid-air and appeared in Saturn's hand, he considered his journal.

At its peak, the journal and all its allies – in each and every one of his realities – had come to have. Still, only one mere purpose, he once believed it was to keep track of his life. Yet, as it turned out, they were to convince himself to do something in another timeline and to have himself for another timeline, persuade himself to do something in the one he had come to know of. A beautifully executed and orchestrated life: that he was the orchestrator of it all. That once, one would have said he had no occupation, even if Saturn was considered as such. Yet he lay awake at night and laboured industriously by day to make his existence ends meet. Travelling in time to execute the plans he had made during his reality.

He was the same person in all his realities. The events had not changed him to be different from each other. And yet, as Saturn held those things in hand, he knew that they were the continuation of some other reality they had once endured in a distant life.

Saturn stood and regarded Arné with deep thought and emotion. For Saturn, it was new. The idea about time which had faced death and exploited time with it. That there in Saturn's hand was a letter, Arné had just written and given to Saturn more than fifty years ago.

Arné walked up to Saturn as he took the note. He knew that a single object could not exist twice in a separate reality and must have disappeared when he completed it. They went down and enjoyed the rest of the celebration.

Epilogue

———

Spring

POV Saturn

Aᶠᵗᵉʳ ᵐʸ ᶜᵒⁿˢᶜⁱᵒᵘˢ ᵐⁱⁿᵈ ʰᵃᵈ drifted back to where I once lay on my deathbed, I reopened my eyes – in eagerness – with a strong will to survive for merely a few minutes to see the triumph of his once long awaiting great expectations. So it was, as it appeared, by some granting miracle in which time had lost its own way. For this beautiful day was both my last day in his future and his first day of my past, ultimately allowing me the inconceivable presence. There I saw him lying silently in his bassinet. And when I smiled, he smiled. And when he cried, I cried. I felt his heartbeat in the palm of my hand like an ever-gentle blossoming flower."

Live well, my gentle souls, for Heaven has prepared a place for you.

THE END

Appendix

Arné's timeline as depicted in the novel

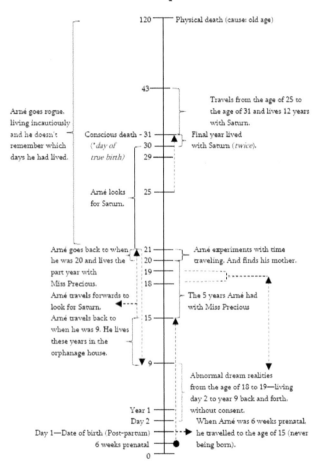

120 —— Physical death (cause: old age)

43 ——

Travels from the age of 25 to
the age of 31 and lives 12 years
with Saturn.

Arné goes rogue,
living incautiously
and he doesn't
remember which
days he had lived.

Conscious death - 31 ——   Final year lived
(*day of   with Saturn (*twice*).
true birth*)   30 ——
29 ——

Arné looks
for Saturn.   25 ——

Arné goes back to when   21 ——   Arné experiments with time
he was 20 and lives the   20 ——   traveling. And finds his mother.
part year with   19 ——
Miss Precious.   18 ——
Arné travels forwards to   The 5 years Arné had
look for Saturn.   with Miss Precious
Arné travels back to   15 ——
when he was 9. He lives
these years in the
orphanage house.

9 ——
Abnormal dream realities
from the age of 18 to 19—living
day 2 to year 9 back and forth,
without consent.

Year 1 ——
Day 2 ——   When Arné was 6 weeks prenatal,
Day 1—Date of birth (Post-partum) ——   he travelled to the age of 15 (never
6 weeks prenatal ——   being born).

0 ——

Author's Notes

A Candle under the Water was first self-published in 2021 under the pseudonym of Réne H.A. Theudric-H. Its November 2023 second edition contains minor editorial changes including the author's real name.

The idea for *A Candle under the Water* had first come to me back when I was in high school. It was in fact after a drive back home from town with my sister. Though the idea had been undeveloped, it lodged inside my consciousness like a seed waiting to be watered. Yet, nothing had come of it for years.

It was not until I was a first-year language student at university when I began thinking of it again. And the very first draft (written with a pen on paper, and less than a hundred pages long) would not appear until the end of that year—2015; completed on an extra bed in my best friend's room in Hermanus, South-Africa.

From there, it took me five more years to edit and rewrite the original manuscript, and not until lockdown 2020, alone in my studio in Strasbourg, France, where I had it completed and ready to send to my father via e-mail in Word format. (Even if I have to admit it myself, his approval and enthusiasm thereof had meant so much to me, to such an extent that I had decided to self-publish it—the project having originally only been something that resembled more of a personal endeavour).

So, towards the end of 2020, I asked my dear friend (and now editor, Jeanne-Mari) to have a look at it, and about three months later she returned it to me, polished. It took me six more months to complete the cover painting and music composition therein, until I had the first two first editions printed via Amazon.

Two months later, re-edited, corrected and published again—six years after I had started working on it; round about ten years since I had originally gotten the idea.

SIT LAVS DEO PATRI

Milton Keynes UK
Ingram Content Group UK Ltd.
UKHW010624291123
433416UK00005B/386